UNLOCKING SECRETS

Keys to Love, Book Two

Kennedy Layne

UNLOCKING SECRETS

Dedication

Jeffrey—Only you hold the secret to my heart...I love you!

Cole—I can't wait for you to unlock the world's secrets! Your college journey is just the beginning!

A grim discovery in Lance Kendall's home proved one thing—the residents of Blyth Lake had a serial killer in their midst. Now Lance had unintentionally put a target on his back. Worst yet, he's made the only woman he ever loved known to a murderer.

A trip down memory lane with the man who'd broken Brynn Mercer's heart wasn't the smartest thing she'd ever done in her life, but their reunion was a slow burn of temptation that she couldn't ignore.

Together, they will only have one chance to correct the past. Will the hidden secrets he uncovered threaten their love or solidify it for a future that has always been out of their reach?

CHAPTER ONE

Twelve years ago…

E MILY STARED INTO the cold dark eyes of a man she should have recognized—only she didn't.

Why did he seem so distant? So far away?

"I-I'm going home," Emma choked out around the nervous constriction in her throat. Fear immobilized her feet to the ground. "Everyone is leaving the party. I've got to get home before my parents find out I'm not in bed."

She ran her sweaty palms down the brand-new pair of ripped jeans she'd bought to impress Billy Stanton. She'd found them on the clearance rack after having saved enough of her allowance to afford them. She wanted to look over her shoulder where the bonfire was still raging, but his unsettling stare kept her from taking her attention off him.

What was he doing here anyway?

Something deeply inherent to her survival told her that she was in danger, but that was impossible. Things like that didn't happen in their small town. He would never really hurt her, right?

"I know I'm late. My mom and dad will freak if they find out I'm late for curfew." Emma wished she'd waited for Brynn or Julie, but it was already an hour past the curfew her parents had initially set up a few years ago. Is that why he was here? Had her parents discovered her empty bed? *Shoot.* That would mean the sheriff was on his way out here and everyone would blame her come Monday morning for the party being busted. "I didn't m-mean to lose track of time."

Emma shifted her weight in unease. He hadn't said a word. Why was he staring at her with such a blank expression?

"Julie and Brynn are right behind me. They'll be here in just a minute."

Emma wasn't sure why she'd lied like that. It wasn't like he didn't know the annual bonfire was taking place and who was in attendance. After all, the alcohol had to be supplied by someone.

His gaze drifted over her shoulders toward the farm.

It wasn't until that moment that she became aware of how still he'd been standing in front of her with his arms hanging down at his sides.

Would he tell her parents where she'd been?

Wait. That didn't make any sense. He'd be in just as much trouble as the rest of them, maybe even more so given the circumstances.

"You're here to warn us, aren't you?"

Relief came over her in waves as she finally connected the dots. She was so stressed about missing curfew that she must have misread the situation.

"My dad called the sheriff, and he's on his way out here, isn't he?" Emma did look over her shoulder, grimacing at the fact that mostly everyone would be grounded come the weekend. They'd all say it was her fault, and Billy would never ask her out. "You should go warn the rest of them. I'll run home and try to make up an excuse as to why I was out so late."

Emma didn't wait around for him to answer. She took off at a dead run, brushing past him as the adrenaline and fear pumped through her at facing the disappointing reaction of her parents.

How could she possibly get out of the grounding of her life?

She ran deeper into the woods, ignoring the rumbling sound of thunder overhead. The gathering clouds made it rather difficult for her to see the path in front of her, but she'd memorized this route from the many times she'd taken it over the years.

The air contained a bit of a chill, especially since she'd been by the bonfire for the last few hours. The only good thing about the fast jog she'd undertaken was that it kept her heartrate up, chasing away the cool breeze stinging her cheeks.

She cried out when the tip of her boot got caught in the root of a tree. The leaves on the ground cushioned her fall, but the palms of her hands still suffered scratches from the coarse sticks littered amongst the foliage. It wasn't her skin she was worried about so much as the condition of the cute little ankle boots she'd borrowed from her sister. If she so much as scuffed the toe, she'd be in deep shit for taking them without asking.

Emma shifted off her hands and knees, choosing to stand instead of sitting on the ground. The clouds took advantage of the moment and slowly covered the moon, limiting the light she'd been using to lead the way. She couldn't see the damage done to her sister's boots, nor the severity of the cuts on her hand. The warm stickiness alerted her to the fact that she was bleeding at least a little.

Was it bad of her to think that she could use this to her advantage? She squinted to try and see how bad the scratches were so she could adjust her story. She could always say she'd fallen on her way home and stopped at Julie's house to clean up the wounds. Would her parents believe her slight misdirection?

Emma didn't have anything to wipe her hands on, but surely she could find something before reaching home.

She flinched when a raindrop hit her cheek. Simultaneously, a low rumble of thunder traveled across the sky. That didn't stop a sliver of moonlight from slipping through the storm clouds...only to reveal a stretched shadow that was coming in her direction.

Emma spun around, surprised to find *him* no more than ten feet away.

"W-what are you doing? Didn't you go and warn the rest of them?"

"Julie and Brynn haven't started walking home yet, have they?"

It sounded more like a statement than a question. Why would he ask her that question?

A sickening sensation rolled her stomach to the point where she physically had to take a step back from the cause.

Something was wrong with him.

He didn't sound like he usually did, always polite and fun to be around.

Why was he acting this way? Was he showing off?

"Y-you don't want to get into trouble, either," Emma pointed out as she struggled to maintain her composure. He was scaring her with his bravado, and she didn't like it. She went on the offensive. "You supplied the keg. I know you did, and so does everyone else that was here tonight."

The man lifted the left side of his mouth as if he were amused by her warning.

It was then she realized she was in trouble...real trouble.

"They couldn't possibly imagine what I'm going to do to you, Emma. They'll all be looking in the wrong direction."

CHAPTER TWO

Present day…

LANCE PUSHED OPEN the lightweight aluminum screened door with his shoulder, carrying three bottles of beer by their necks in one hand while holding a paper plate containing his extra-large slice of fresh apple pie in the other. The sweet aroma of sugar and cinnamon had been too much to resist. There was no doubt he would regret this decision later when he finally got around to running off the additional calories.

"Where are you fitting that?" The disbelief was evident in his brother's tone as Lance handed over two of the bottles in his grip. "Those Delmonico ribeye steaks Dad grilled could have fed a platoon for a week, and that doesn't even include the baked potatoes that were the size of a grapefruit and the other sides. I shouldn't have had that damned tossed salad first. I might have had enough room left to fit a slice of that pie after eating a whole side of beef."

Noah wasn't exaggerating. Their dad had gone all out with this homecoming dinner, including all the trimmings, but Lance wouldn't have wanted it any other way. Sitting and digesting a home-cooked meal on Dad's porch overlooking the old homestead was a tradition worth continuing, providing the beer held out.

He'd been gone for twelve long years serving his country, visiting home only when time between deployments allowed.

Even though he was a year younger than Noah, they'd both entered the Marines around the same time.

The only difference between the two was that Lance had graduated high school a full year early and his enlistment had been on the delayed entry program—not that he ever rubbed that in Noah's face at every turn in the road.

Lance had always taken issue with being the youngest of five siblings, running up behind them on every outing they would let him tag along on. He, his brothers, and his sister shared a healthy competition in everything they'd done—including honoring their family legacy of serving their country. They served because freedom wasn't free, and they didn't ride the coattails of better men. No one would ever find a Kendall in Macalister County who would stand for one second being in another man's debt.

Noah wasn't going to ruin this apple pie moment for Lance.

"I've been living off nothing but the chow hall and fast food for the last couple of months," Lance reminded Noah wryly before taking a seat in one of the wicker chairs opposite him. The floral cushion reminded him that his mother hadn't been part of the welcoming committee.

She was missed.

Her absence was profound, but she would want them to carry on as the strong young men and woman they were raised to be.

"Cut me some slack. Besides, didn't this apple pie come from Annie's Diner? I wouldn't want Ms. Osburn to find out I skipped out on her homemade all-American dessert."

Noah shared a sideways glance with the beautiful woman sitting next to him, though it wasn't unexpected. This had been an ongoing regular occurrence between the two of them all evening.

Lance wouldn't deny that he'd been surprised to drive up to the family homestead to find his father and brother in the company of a petite brunette he'd never laid his eyes on before tonight. His interest had been immediately piqued by her beauty and intellect. All his brothers and sister had made a pact to never bring anyone home who they weren't serious about in the long run. It was another tradition that they had all unofficially endorsed.

That meant Reese Woodward was one very special lady.

Lance took the moment of awkward silence to enjoy his ice-cold beer, his large slice of apple pie, and the warm summer evening he'd been dreaming about for the last three years. It was at his mother's funeral that the Kendall siblings had all made the decision to finally come home, deciding not to ride their enlistments out for the full twenty and retirement.

His mouth watered the instant the warm cinnamon and sugary apples hit his taste buds.

Damn, it was good to be home after all those deployments.

It was the first of August and rather humid in Ohio, but nothing compared to the dry heat of south central Afghanistan. Hell, he hadn't seen one lightning bug in that whole damned sandbox, nor had he heard the soothing sounds of crickets and frogs as he fell asleep under stars not so different from his own nights here at home.

No.

He'd had to get accustomed to waking up to the hissing sounds of inbound mortars overhead, feeling that telltale vibration in the ground with their impact and muted detonation. Of course, those were just precursors to their own meaty cracks followed by distant thuds of well-targeted outgoing Howitzer projectiles hitting the ground to lull him back into slumber.

It wasn't something he'd ever miss.

Lance allowed the welcoming resonances that most people took for granted to wash over him. He inhaled deeply as he leaned back against his mom's cushions and savored the fragrance of the tea roses planted in the front yard.

These small tea roses called Darlow's Enigma had been one of his mother's favorite flowers. The sweet scent alone let him know that she was here with them in spirit. Their thorns reminded him of her wit.

"Ms. Osburn didn't make that pie, Lance. She rarely does any of the cooking at the diner anymore."

Damn it.

Couldn't his brother have waited until he'd finished this slice of way-past-due delicious dessert before crushing his dreams?

Lance let his fork drop to the plate with a disappointed look on his brow.

Noah laid an arm over the back of the cushion as he got down to business. Couldn't his brother see that Lance wasn't the only one who could have used a little more time to enjoy the evening? Reese had become somewhat antsy at where this discussion was headed, and though Lance realized they'd put it off too long, another five minutes of peace wouldn't have hurt anyone.

Noah always did have to play the killjoy. It appeared it was finally time to deal with what had thrown every resident in Blyth Lake for a loop.

"Can we at least start at the beginning?" Lance asked in defeat, wishing their father would come outside to join them. It was like being in direct line of fire without someone at least having his six. "Reese, you came to Blyth Lake hoping to find out about the time your cousin attended camp here, is that right?"

"Yes." Reese shot Noah a sad smile that spoke volumes of

how her journey had ended. "I found a photograph of Sophia and Emma Irwin together that summer. It was taken a few months before Emma went missing. I'd recalled hearing about her disappearance when I was younger, but I never made any connection to Sophia until I'd found the picture when I was visiting home last Christmas."

The connection Reese had made was the fact that Emma Irwin and Sophia Morton had disappeared exactly one year apart. Their hometowns were approximately thirty miles away. Unfortunately, no one else had tied the cases together because Sophia had been listed in the papers as a probable runaway.

"I'm sorry about your cousin, Reese." Lance extended his condolences, though he could only imagine the grief her family must have endured. Even he easily recalled the girl's radiant smile and infectious laugh from the small amount of time he'd spent with her twelve years ago. "She was a nice girl from what I remember."

Lance leaned forward and set his half-eaten slice of pie onto the glass top of the matching wicker table. Everyone had the same type reaction anytime the name Emma Irwin was brought up in conversation. Her disappearance had rocked the town, eventually causing her family to move away from the speculation of what might have happened during that fated October.

Now it seemed that Emma and Sophia did have a connection...in death.

"Emma was in the same grade as I was back in high school. Hell, we'd grown up together. I can still remember waking up to Chad Schaeffer banging on the front door of the house to tell us we needed to join the search party for Emma."

"I remember that morning," Noah said, almost as if he'd forgotten. That was impossible, though. Every resident in Blyth Lake had combed every square inch of the town that day.

Unfortunately, Emma had never been found. "Mitch and Gwen had already left home to enlist in their respective services. Mom called each of them at their duty stations that same day so they wouldn't hear the news from anyone else. As for Jace, he was sick that summer with mono and couldn't join in the search. They had all been close to Emma's older sister, Shae."

Lance truly wished he had the answers Reese was seeking, but he'd been seventeen years old that summer.

"I know you want to ask me questions about the two weeks I spent at the camp with Emma and Sophia, but can we cover the events of the last two months first?" Lance had received a call from a state police detective about a body being discovered in a wall of Noah's new residence. To say he was surprised was an understatement. "Noah, you bought the old Yoder place? And in the process of remodeling, you discovered a body?"

Lance was beginning to think he should have stayed away from home for another month or two. This type of homecoming wasn't exactly welcoming.

Noah lowered his leg from where his ankle had been resting on his other knee. It was easy to see that he was uncomfortable with Lance's question. Hell, he would be too if he'd taken a sledge hammer to a wall, only to uncover a partially mummified corpse who he thought was Emma Irwin.

Unfortunately, the body had turned out to be none other than Sophia Morton. That discovery had turned them all on their heads.

"Something like that," Noah hedged, glancing toward the front door where their father had yet to make an appearance. "You know that Phil Yoder died years ago, prompting his family to leave the area and Pete Anderson to buy the land at auction. Well, the Andersons added a small office between the living room and the open kitchen. Reese was helping me take down the wall when we discovered Sophia's body. Granted, we thought it was Emma—like everyone else did—all along until the DNA results came in."

Lance didn't miss the way Reese winced at the summation of events. It hadn't been his intention to upset her with his need to know the timeline of the last few months, but it would certainly come in handy when he spoke to Detective Kendrick in person tomorrow morning at the diner.

Lance was being drawn into Sophia's homicide investigation all because he'd attended summer camp with her twelve years before.

Honestly, Lance could only imagine the shock Reese had experienced upon finding out that her cousin hadn't run away from home at all, but instead had been murdered and stuffed into a wall to be forgotten for all time.

And for her to be one of the two to find her body?

It was incomprehensible.

What Lance really wanted to ask was how Noah could live in a house after such a discovery, but he kept that opinion to himself. Noah always did see the glass as half full, and no doubt truly believed his acquisition of the Yoder property had been in the cards in order for Sophia's family to gain some semblance of closure after all these years.

Noah had an odd way of looking at things.

"Lance, could I see you for a moment?"

Gus Kendall stepped onto the lighted porch, holding the screened door open for his youngest son to follow his directive. Dusk had fallen without Lance realizing how much time they'd spent talking about this past summer. He, Noah, and Reese still had a lot of ground to cover, especially before he met with Detective Kendrick.

Family came first, though.

Noah was already nodding his approval, his not-so-innocent gesture telling Lance that his brother was already in the know about what their father wanted to discuss in private. Being summoned by their dad for a private chat wasn't usually a good thing. At least, in his experience.

"Of course," Lance responded, shooting Noah an expression of gratitude for the heads up. It most likely had to do with his future. Out of all the siblings in the Kendall clan, he'd been the only one who'd shown an interest in their father's work. "I'll see you two tomorrow?"

"Hopefully *before* you meet with Detective Kendrick," Noah answered, taking Reese's hand as the two of them stood to make their way back to the Yoder farm. Only it wasn't the Yoder's or the Anderson's property anymore. It was Noah's place. "We haven't covered even half of what transpired in the last few weeks alone."

Lance didn't bother to tell Noah that their father had filled in all the details, down to the fact that Reese had almost been run out of town for reasons that had nothing to do with Sophia's murder or Emma's disappearance.

"Seven sharp at the diner?"

"Make it eight," Noah replied, once again causing Lance's curiosity to rise regarding the knowing looks that had passed between his brother, Reese, and his father. "Good luck."

Good luck?

What the hell did that crap mean?

Reese's dimple gave away that the two of them were still withholding vital information, but whatever it was must be on the good side of things. It didn't take a genius to figure out it had to do with his upcoming talk with Dad. Lance gathered his empty beer bottle and the plate still containing his half-eaten pie. Noah could pick up his own damn trash.

"Come on inside, son."

"Noah," Lance called out, gathering the courage to hold up a finger to stall their dad. That had never gone over well when they were younger. He lowered his voice so that Gus couldn't overhear their exchange. "Is he retiring? Tell me now so that I don't look like a fish that's been taken out of water. I'm not quite ready to take on the entire family business by myself."

"You're on your own there, buddy."

Noah's laughter could be heard all the way until he'd reached his F150, opening the passenger side door for Reese. It was then that Lance realized his brother had left him to pick up their empty bottles.

Son of a bitch.

When had he become their maid?

"Do you remember your Grandpa Earl?" Gus asked, allowing the screen door to close behind Lance as he juggled all the garbage from the porch. The central air was working overtime, but it was a nice change from the humidity outside. "He used to give each of you kids a silver dollar when he came to Sunday dinner."

"No," Lance argued, walking through the dining room and down the small hall that led to the kitchen. Again, the absence of his mother hit him right in the gut. The walls were lined with family photographs. His father had a fresh-cut bouquet of small white roses with bright golden centers in a vase on the dining room table. His mother would usually use lilacs as a centerpiece in the spring and would switch to the tea roses later in the summer. Nothing in the house had been changed, and her memory lived on. "Mom always let it slide, but us boys weren't too happy to find out that Gwen always got two silver coins from Grandpa. No wonder she became a financial planner. She received her inheritance early. Her portfolio alone could probably allow her to retire by now."

Lance entered the kitchen, recycling what he could before rinsing his fork in the sink and dropping it into a glass half full of water that still needed to be put into the dishwasher. There were some things that were just ingrained from childhood. He would pitch in around the house as best he could while staying here. He'd find a piece of property just like Noah had, though Lance had yet to make a call to the town's realtor.

He was allowing himself a little downtime before deciding what to do with his life, but hopefully the upcoming conversation could shed a little light on his future. He'd love to work with his father making furniture by hand, the old-fashioned way. The kitchen table was the perfect example of the type of craftsmanship that wasn't seen in today's furniture.

Lance wanted to be a part of that hands-on creation.

"Gwen had Earl wrapped around her little finger," Gus agreed with a fond laugh, sitting at the kitchen table Lance would like to replicate for his own house one day. "Take a seat, son."

Lance didn't have the best of memories when it came to that saying, and they usually involved his brothers. He still didn't regret daring Noah to steal one of their father's beers out of the refrigerator. The recollection brought a smile to his face, regardless that they'd both been grounded for a whole week during one of their summer breaks.

"This isn't about your health, is it?" Lance was relatively sure this upcoming discussion had nothing to do with his father's heart condition based on Noah's behavior this evening, but then again, he could have misread the signs. "Have you been doing what your heart specialist told you to do?"

"My ticker is working just fine, thank you," Gus said dryly with a shake of his head. "What is it with you and Noah thinking

I'm ready to keel over at any moment?"

Lance wasn't sure what to say to that, so he did the smart thing and remained quiet. He pulled out one of the chairs at the table and took a seat with relief. Maybe this did have to do with going into business with his dad.

"We just worry about you, is all," Lance assured him, thinking he should have poured himself a cup of coffee from the pot his father had brewed after dinner. "You brought up Grandpa Earl. Does this have to do with Uncle Jimmy and all that crap?"

"Let's not discuss your mother's brother just now." Gus crossed his arms over his chest and got right down to business. "When your grandfather died, he left your mother quite a healthy inheritance at that time."

This was news to Lance. A healthy inheritance? They'd all had a decent upbringing, but material wealth hadn't been handed to any of them. Gus Kendall was a very proud man, in many ways. He'd always prided himself on providing for his wife and children. At times, this had caused a little dissention between their father and grandfather.

"Now, Earl and I didn't always see eye to eye on things, especially when it came to your mother."

Lance rubbed his upper lip to hide the fact that he was smiling at such a declaration. Gus was certainly putting that sentiment mildly.

"What mattered was that the two of you put away your differences for Mom's sake." Lance could still picture Mary Kendall bustling around the kitchen singing one of her favorite Elvis songs as she cooked Sunday dinner. It was her favorite day of the week. "You made her very happy. Of that, I'm sure Grandpa was well aware."

"It was the other way around, Lance. She made me the happiest man alive." Gus stared into the depth of his coffee cup as if he were watching a movie of his life play out before him. It tore Lance's heart in two to see his father grieve over the love of his life. He cleared his throat before continuing. "Anyway, your mother and I never touched a dime of that inheritance, though it was hers to do with as she wished when she wanted."

Gus set his coffee down on one of the yellow placemats his mother had chosen years ago, leaning forward for a set of keys on a silver ring. He took his time removing a smaller set from the larger array, allowing Lance time to try and figure out the direction this conversation was taking.

He was absolutely clueless thus far.

"It was her final wish to have all you kids home, living close to one another so your children experienced a childhood like yours. She passed before we could choose all the properties together, so I took it upon myself to follow through with her request."

"Dad, you're not saying—"

"I'm saying that Noah was given the Yoder's farm. You're being gifted with the old Fetter property for your part, and the others will be given theirs upon their homecoming. I want this kept quiet from them, you understand? They're going to find out the same way you did."

"Yes, sir," Lance muttered, utterly speechless to say anything after those two words.

Gus quietly set a small ring of identical keys in front of Lance before replacing the larger one with the remaining set back on the Lazy Susan in the center of the table. He then settled back into his chair and gave Lance time to absorb the news of this amazing gift.

Lance was being honored with his mother's last wish—a home to call his own.

He would have given anything to have Mary Kendall standing here in this kitchen with her husband to present him with such an offering.

"Noah was given the Yoder's property."

That would explain some things, especially his brother's need to stay in the house chosen for him. Lance would have done the exact same thing given the circumstances.

"This key is to your new home. Now, don't get too excited. Arthur Fetter let the house become rather rundown over the years, so there's a lot of repairs and outright reconstruction projects in your future, but the bones of the place are all solid. We can swing by your home first thing in the morning and check for hidden bodies and such." Gus' small smile disappeared as he pushed back his chair and stood, taking his coffee with him. He gently rested his weathered hand on Lance's shoulder. "Welcome home, son."

CHAPTER THREE

"**H**AVE YOU HEARD that Lance Kendall is back in town?"

Brynn caught the shot glass she'd been polishing before she dropped it on the floor. It was a good thing her back was toward Jeremy Bell and Miles Schaeffer, or else the fact that their news affected her so dramatically would have been all over town come morning.

The bar was rather busy for a Wednesday night, but she chalked that up to all the media crews in town and their propensity to drink themselves into a stupor. The local B&B hadn't been sold out of rooms like they currently were since Cindy Lou's wedding. That had to be going on four years now, especially considering her son was turning four years old.

The bass of the country music coming out of the jukebox was at the right intensity that the patrons could enjoy their conversations with a mild level of privacy. Every now and then the smack of a cue ball was followed up with a yell of victory, and the clanking of glasses signified a celebration was fulfilling its purpose.

"Let's hope Lance has better luck with his new house than Noah did with the Yoder place."

"Hey, that's confidential information," Harlan warned Miles, though he wouldn't have had to say anything if he'd kept his mouth shut in the first place. That was the problem with small towns, but she honestly wouldn't live anywhere else than here in

Blyth Lake. "I'm sure Gus is handing over the keys as we speak, but make sure you act surprised when Lance comes strolling in here with his dad later."

Lance Kendall.

He'd been the star running back of the football team back in high school.

He had also been the only boy who had ever broken her heart.

"Brynn, didn't you used to date that Kendall boy?" Jeremy asked, waiting for her to turn around to face them before sliding his empty beer bottle her way. Brynn silently counted how many he'd had this evening, figuring he was due a few more before she would give his daughter a call to ferry him home. "Whitney always had a thing for Billy Stanton, but I remember her saying that you and Lance went to prom your senior year."

"It was homecoming, actually," Brynn corrected him with a smile, maintaining a carefree tone so that no one was the wiser that this conversation was akin to driving a stake into her heart. It wasn't that she was still hung up on Lance. Too much time had gone by to still hold a grudge. "He graduated early to go into the Marines, remember?"

"You're right," Miles said with a nod of agreement. He leaned back on his bar stool and called out to his youngest son. "Chad, did you know that Lance Kendall is back in town?"

Chad was playing darts with Irish, both of them high off their win in the annual county championship battle. Chad had come in first, with Irish second. All that mattered to either of them was that they'd put Billy Stanton in his place—third. Billy was finally finding out that money couldn't buy him the county championship title.

Chad held up his hand to indicate that he would come join his father in a minute, obviously not wanting to break his concentration.

"Did you know that Lance has a meeting with Detective Kendrick at nine o'clock tomorrow morning at the diner?"

"Where are you getting this information, Jeremy?" Harlan asked before checking his phone. His wife must be calling to find out why he wasn't home for dinner. "Has Whitney been in contact with Lance?"

"Nah," Jeremy answered with an impatient wave of his hand, "that girl is too busy with that no-good boy she hooked up with a few months back. I was at the diner earlier and overheard that pretty news anchor from Channel Five going over her schedule. Trust me, she'll be at the diner tomorrow morning trying to get a scoop on the other media crews in town. Not that Lance would have anything to tell her, though."

Brynn collected Harlan's empty glass, tossing the ice he always requested into his Screwdriver. He was one of the few patrons who preferred his drink with cubes.

She continued to listen in on the various conversations around the bar. Most of the stories revolved around the Kendall siblings returning home after being gone for twelve or more years. Mitch was the oldest, and Brynn figured he was at least five years older than the rest. After him came Gwen, Jace, and then Noah. Lance was the youngest of the clan, though he was mature beyond his years due to growing up circulating in the same circles as all his brothers and sister. Him leaving Blyth Lake to honor his family's legacy proved that point beyond a shadow of a doubt.

"Doesn't the discovery of Sophia Morton's body make you wonder what really happened to Emma Irwin?"

Brynn's heart twisted upon hearing her friend's name. Emma had never been so happy as she'd been that fateful night. She'd been ecstatic that Billy Stanton had danced with her by the bonfire, going so far as to say she thought Billy would ask her out for the following weekend. Even the chance of getting caught sneaking into her house past curfew couldn't chase away her bright smile.

The weeks following had been nothing less than an emotional rollercoaster.

How could a seventeen-year-old girl up and disappear into thin air? She couldn't. That meant there had been some sort of foul play.

The days turned into weeks, the weeks into months, and eventually months into years. Hope began to evaporate little by little until there had been nothing left.

"Brynn?"

She'd gotten sucked into the past, which was happening a lot lately, and she wasn't quite sure how long Tiny had been calling her name.

"I thought you were taking Rose into the city tonight?" Brynn asked before taking another glance around the bar to see if anyone else needed another drink. She swiped Miles' empty draft beer glass out for a full one. "You shouldn't be back quite yet, Tiny."

The man she adored more than any other male on the face of the earth stood at six feet and six inches tall. He was African American with the brightest smile that could make the worst day better with just a flash. He'd shaved his head long ago, claiming that he wasn't going to give away his age.

She didn't care how old he was or that he didn't have a single hair on top of his head.

He was her protector. He and his wife, Rose, had taken her in at the young age of fifteen years old when she didn't have any other place to go. They had both seen to it that she stayed in school and out of trouble when all she'd wanted to do was run away from facing the death of her parents.

"There was some trouble up at the lake." Tiny took the dishtowel from her hand and proved that old habits die hard. "Deputy Foster caught some teenagers partying in one of the empty cottages. It's all taken care of now, but she's personally paying a visit to each of the parents as we speak."

"Now why doesn't that surprise me?" Brynn asked with a laugh, taking back the dishtowel and trying unsuccessfully to chase him out from behind the bar. "Would you go and relax? You don't have to work the bar anymore. It's my job now."

"I know that," Tiny agreed, though his actions said something else entirely when he started to roll up his sleeves. "There's nothing wrong with another person helping out, you know."

Brynn had known all along that even though she'd purchased the bar—known as Tiny's Cavern to the locals—Tiny would never be able to fully relinquish his hold on the old stomping ground.

She honestly didn't mind, and the support Tiny and Rose had shown her over the years was more than she could have ever asked for in regard to this new path she'd chosen over leaving Blyth Lake. She'd always known it would be the natural continuation of that storyline. They were her family, and this town was her home.

"You're here because you heard Lance was back in town," Brynn said, handing him off a glass so that he could dry it before storing it back in the rack. She might as well take advantage of his presence, seeing as he refused to go join some of his friends over by the pool table. "That was a long time ago, Tiny."

"That it was," Tiny agreed, though his warm eyes still held a hint of skepticism at the ease of which she'd addressed the elephant in the room. Even the patrons weren't ignoring the big grey animal. "He still broke your heart."

"And I believe I broke his." Brynn wasn't saying that seeing Lance again wouldn't be hard, but time, understanding, and acceptance played a big part in forgiveness. "He never lied to me, Tiny. Everyone in town knew that every Kendall sibling would sign on the dotted line to serve their country. I was well aware of that fact."

"He asked you to wait for him," Tiny reminded her gently, as if she couldn't recall each and every word of their final conversation. Well, final as far as being a couple. They tried being friends after his departure and had even exchanged letters for the first six months he'd left town. Contact between them eventually faded as she went to a community college a few towns over and Lance was shipped out for his first deployment. "You could have said yes."

Yes, she could have, but then their lives wouldn't have turned out the same. Lance most likely would have tried to get her to move to all the various places he'd been stationed, leaving her with no support. She'd been there and done that with her biological parents. They had never been there for her, and unfortunately, their deaths hadn't shown her any differently.

The only thing good to come out of such a tragedy had been Tiny and Rose. Brynn had found a family with them, and she wouldn't have given that up for anything in the world.

She'd chosen to stay in Blyth Lake, and there wasn't a single day that passed that she regretted her choice.

That didn't mean Lance hadn't crossed her mind from time to time. He'd been her first love.

"Go join Chester for a round of pool," Brynn suggested, giving Tiny a playful shove that didn't move him an inch. "He's been itching to play you ever since you cleaned the table in one round."

"He'll still be there in an hour. We both know that."

It was obvious that Tiny wasn't going to budge on helping her out tonight. She sighed in resignation, leaving him to join in the conversation with Jeremy and Miles regarding Emma Irwin and Sophia Morton. Personally, Brynn couldn't take hearing any more about Sophia's body being discovered in the wall of Noah Kendall's home.

She lifted the small section of the bar that Tiny had managed to fit his large body through, setting it down behind her before heading toward the back to make sure that the restrooms didn't need restocked. It would be one less thing she would have to do come closing time.

"Brynn Mercer? Would you mind if I asked you a couple of questions?"

Brynn somehow managed to suppress a groan of irritation when the annoying redhead of Channel Five News decided now would be good time to ask questions regarding the very same topic she was trying to avoid.

"I'm sorry." Brynn tossed the woman a small smile to soften the refusal. "Now isn't a good time."

"This will only take a minute, I promise." Charlene Winston rested her manicured nails on Brynn's forearm to stop her from walking away. "It's come to my attention that you used to be best friends with Emma Irwin. Did you know that she'd forged a friendship with Sophia Morton? Do you think their cases are connected?"

"I have no comment," Brynn managed to say around the tight constriction of her throat. "Please excuse me."

Everyone in town thought there was a connection, but Charlene Winston's questions were just bait for a soundbite on tonight's eleven o'clock news. Brynn wouldn't stoop to that level for a bit of fame.

Hell, she'd had her fifteen minutes in the limelight after her parents' deaths. She wasn't inclined to seek the notoriety of being the latest news story ever again.

"What about Lance Kendall? It's my understanding that he used to date both you and Sophia. Don't you think it's more than a coincidence that Noah Kendall was the one to find Sophia Morton's body?"

Brynn wasn't a physical type person, by any means. She'd always been one to avoid confrontations, except when needed. Her frame was rather small with her only standing at five feet and five inches tall, and she became nauseous at the sight of blood.

That didn't mean she would allow some stranger to come into town and make allegations that could ruin a good man's reputation.

That wasn't going to happen, and it was time someone stepped up to the plate.

Brynn could easily hear the gasps and exclamations of shock from the numerous patrons who'd come into the Cavern to relax and shed the stress of their day over the bass of the jukebox. She'd instinctively backed Charlene Winston against the wall and pointed a finger in her face so the woman didn't miss a word of the advice she was about to receive.

"If I so much as hear another disparaging word come out of your mouth about the Kendall family, I will personally make a call to your superiors to let them know about the drug problem you are so obviously struggling with," Brynn muttered threateningly, stepping even closer when Charlene tried to slip away from the wall. "You see, that white powder on your face has nothing to do with the caked-on makeup you use to go live on camera. This comes down to karma, Ms. Winston. You tarnish the Kendalls' surname around here, and I will do the same to you at the network headquarters."

Brynn waited until Charlene slowly nodded her acceptance of what would happen should she utter one word against the Kendalls before stepping back and allowing the woman room to draw a breath.

Everyone consistently underestimated the petite blonde who hadn't always had it easy and worked in a bar. Maybe Charlene Winston knew Brynn owned the place or maybe she didn't, but the woman would sure enough remember the warning being issued and be very careful before throwing slander on the residents of Blyth Lake.

CHAPTER FOUR

"**M**OM, I SURE hope you're listening."

Lance sat on the porch of his new home as his father drove down the lane toward town. Dust swirled behind the tailgate in a beautiful pattern that only an old gravel road in the country could create. He finally understood what his dad meant when he used to say that only people who had been away from everything they loved could appreciate the small details when their world reappeared.

Upon returning from Iraq and Afghanistan, Lance had experienced many of the same emotions—an appreciation for life on a small stage.

Even flushing toilets had become a scene of wonder. Most individuals would never know how good they had it here. Life in small town America was as sweet as fresh honey from the hive.

He looked forward to the day when he didn't feel like he had to have a weapon by his side to feel whole. Until that day came, he would have to make some arrangements to renew his carry permit now that he'd returned from active duty abroad and currently had a new home address.

Home—twelve acres of spacious land, the large barn positioned to the south that had seen much better days, and the quintessential two-story farmhouse with a complete basement. All of these things were now his—a place to call his own.

Lance wasn't sure he could put into words what this mo-

ment meant to him, but it seemed appropriate that he try. He'd
already thanked his dad and had been given the grand tour of the
old Fetter place.

From this moment forward, it would be known as Lance
Kendall's property.

"I can't even begin to tell you how much I miss you." Lance
ran a hand over the worn wood of the porch, picking a weed
that had come up through the planks. "It honestly didn't seem
real to drive into town, knowing you wouldn't be standing on
the front porch with a dishtowel in your hand to usher us inside
for a home-cooked meal once we returned. Don't get me wrong.
Dad did his best to fill your shoes, but let's face it—he certainly
doesn't give hugs the way you do. As a matter of fact, I'm pretty
sure I still have the imprint of his hand on my back."

Mary Kendall had always been full of life and just a phone
call away. That first year Lance had left home had been a hard
row to hoe. Marine Corps Recruit Training had been no picnic.
That bit of hell had been followed by ITS and then Camp
Pendleton as his first duty station.

It wasn't something any of the Kendalls talked about over
family meals. Honestly, serving their country was just what the
Kendalls did and everyone followed in those footsteps. But
Lance sure as hell called home to talk to his mama every chance
he got, because she was the only one who could make everything
okay even when she was thousands of miles away.

"This..." Lance let his voice trail off as he swept his gaze
across what was now his land. "This is more than I could have
ever imagined, Mama. These gifts you gave to us will eventually
be handed down to your grandchildren and then your great-
grandchildren. You've brought us home, bought us homes, and I
am so sorry that you're not here in person to witness our
homecoming."

Lance would never admit it aloud, but he was envious that Mitch had gotten five additional years with their mother. One thing he'd learned over the last twelve years was that time was precious. The small things mattered more than anyone knew.

"I will not disappoint you, Mama."

All it had taken Lance was a brief moment after walking through the front door of his new home to envision what it would be like come the end of the year. He'd even picked out the bay window in the living room facing the driveway as the perfect place to put his Christmas tree. His mother had loved the scent of evergreens, so much so that the road leading to the family homestead was lined with full-bodied blue spruce trees Dad trimmed each year before the Christmas season.

The low hum of an engine cut through the peaceful morning, signaling his brother's impatience for the talk they'd postponed last night.

"Oh, and Mama?" Lance lifted a hand in greeting as Noah pulled his truck in beside Lance's beat-up old silver F-150 that needed a few days in the shop. He couldn't bring himself to part with his first owned vehicle, and it had nothing to do with not having a car payment. "I really appreciate you looking out for me. I wouldn't have done so well finding a body in the wall of my house. I speak on behalf of the rest of us when I say we're all glad it was Noah."

"Hey," Noah called out as he stepped out of his much newer F-150. "I just passed Dad, and he said you were still here. Hard to believe these old places are our new digs, huh?"

"You knew about Mom's final wish since you got back to town and you didn't warn me?" Lance was only half-serious, especially after the warning Gus had issued this morning about keeping these new homes under wraps. "I'm pretty sure you owe me breakfast."

"Congratulations, brother."

Lance stood and accepted Noah's handshake, feigning this was like every other morning. Had they each let emotions override this moment, neither one would make it into town for breakfast. Biscuits and gravy were sounding pretty good right about now.

"Do you remember old man Fetter?" Lance asked, leading the way up the porch steps and into the house. This place wouldn't require a total renovation like Noah's house, but it certainly hadn't been updated since the '70s. "I never in a million years thought he'd leave Blyth Lake."

"I didn't even know he'd moved to Florida to be with his daughter until a few days ago when Chester mentioned his weekly Euchre card game was short on players." Noah ran his hand over the chair rail in the living room. "You could sand this down and revert it back to its original look."

"It wasn't part of the initial design, though. Look. This one over here is already falling off." Lance didn't use a bit of strength when he touched the chair rail near the door. It fell to the floor with a thud. "Did Chester rope you into playing cards?"

"I was waiting for you, Mitch, Jace, and Gwen to show up so that we can start our own weekly card game," Noah replied with a smile. "And trust me, we won't be playing Euchre."

Uncle Jimmy taught his niece and nephews how to play dealer's choice poker when they were younger, so each of them were rather well-versed in the various forms of the game. It made for interesting stakes, considering they all knew each other's tells. With Reese in the mix, well, that could make things even more interesting.

"Where's Reese?" Lance followed Noah through the house, allowing his brother to take stock of the work ahead. It went unspoken that they would help each other over the next few months and years after that with never-ending renovations, just as they would help the others in restoring their homes. Though they might be living in separate residences, their parents had seen to it that Blyth Lake was their home. "I thought she'd be with you to finish the conversation from last night."

"She's at an interview with one of the high school adminis-trators and a schoolboard member. She's looking at taking a teaching position at our alma mater." Noah surveyed the main and upper floors before opening the basement door located off the kitchen. He flipped the light switch and bathed the descend-ing stairwell in a golden hue. "I'm surprised that these steps are in such good shape."

"Be careful," Lance warned him, having already visited the cold damp cellar earlier. "There's enough cobwebs down there to house a thousand or so spiders. First thing I'm gonna do is bug bomb this place until the walls glow. How's Reese doing, anyway? It couldn't have been easy to find out that the body belonged to Sophia."

"It wasn't. And I've got to tell you, the suspect pool isn't all that big considering who had access to the Yoder's farmhouse back in the day."

Noah carefully descended the steps one at a time until he'd reached the bottom. He found the dangling string to the lone lightbulb easily, but Lance had plans to rewire the electricity down here for more access to lighting and power outlets.

Most folks in Ohio used their basements as storm shelters during tornado season. Lance wanted additional amenities down here to make it more habitable, plus he'd need a place to work and store his weapons.

Lance pondered what Noah meant by the suspect pool, but it didn't take a genius to figure out whoever put Sophia's body behind that drywall was connected to the Andersons in some form or fashion.

Lance had been seventeen years old at the time Emma went missing, so that meant he would have been eighteen and already through boot camp before Pete Anderson put up that wall. Unfortunately, that led him to believe they all personally knew whomever it was who had committed such a horrifying act.

"Originally, Detective Kendrick found out that you were the one who snuck out Emma and Sophia from the campground the summer before Emma went missing." Noah circled the basement while Lance took a seat on one of the lower steps. He could see why Noah had driven out here instead of having this conversation in town. Gossip was rife in these small towns, and Blyth Lake was no exception. "Kendrick thought there might be a connection until Ms. Osburn clarified what happened that night for everyone."

"Sophia practically begged me to drive her into town, especially after Emma's sister refused to take the chance of getting caught." Lance had to smile at the lengths Sophia and Emma had gone to in order to get a ride into town. "She'd promised to be the one to cover for me and Brynn Mercer when we went skinny dipping. You know how Birdie was about those kinda things."

That had been a night he would never forget. And he still didn't regret taking the chance of being caught in town by his parents. Any time spent with Brynn back then had been worth the grounding of a lifetime.

"Yeah, well, did you ever ask why Sophia wanted to go into town?"

"Noah, I was given the chance to go skinny dipping with a girl I'd had a crush on all through junior high and high school. I wasn't asking questions." Lance really shouldn't have to explain this to Noah, especially considering he had Byron Warner—who had been five years older—buy a bottle of strawberry wine to impress Whitney Bell. On second thought, that hadn't turned out all that well. "I honestly didn't care to know why Sophia and Emma wanted to go into town. I parked on Seventh Street by the cemetery so that no one would see my truck. Those two walked to Main Street from there and came back around forty-five minutes later. I explained all this to Detective Kendrick on the phone, but he still wants to meet with me in person."

Lance had come to find out from the state detective that Sophia had set her mind on talking with Annie Osburn, the woman who owned the diner. It turned out that Annie had been an actress years before, returning to Blyth Lake with a daughter in tow, and Sophia had high hopes that the woman would give her advice on how to break into the acting business.

Noah and Reese had filled in the gaps from there, though not regarding Sophia. As far as anyone knew after the camp, no one had heard from Sophia Morton again. Everyone had carried on with their lives, or so everyone had thought.

What surprised Lance was to discover that Reese coming to Blyth Lake for answers had prompted Annie Osburn's daughter to panic at the thought of someone finding out about her mother's not-so-reputable start in Hollywood. Cassie Osburn had gone to severe lengths to chase Reese out of town before secrets had been spilled.

"Pete Anderson claims he was the one who put up that additional wall...without a body being stuffed inside the drywall." Noah had done a full circle and was currently leaning against the wooden railing of the staircase. It was then that Lance saw the stress of the last few months in his brother's features. "I believe him when he said he did the work."

"Did Detective Kendrick share with you the coroner's report?"

"Sophia *was* killed eleven years ago." Noah rubbed a hand down his face in frustration. "Somehow, someway, her body was put into that wall without Pete Anderson's knowledge during construction."

Lance didn't have to tell Noah that his speculation seemed a bit far-fetched. What did seem plausible was the belief that Emma Irwin had suffered a similar fate.

"I can already see where your mind is going, and the answer is yes." Noah didn't seem to be in any hurry to leave for town, so Lance leaned back on the step behind him to rest his elbows. "My property was scoured by the state forensics team for anything and everything. And you can bet your ass that when they were done, I still searched every inch of that house. Oh, and they also dragged the pond. Emma was nowhere to be found."

"What about the graveyard?" It had been a long drive from Oceanside, California to Blyth Lake, Ohio, so Lance had quite a bit of time to think about the current events on the trip home. "Wouldn't the cemetery be the perfect burial ground to hide a body? Were there any burials around the time that Emma disappeared?"

"That's real sick, you know that?" Noah shook his head in disgust as he pulled the whitish-grey string to plunge the basement into darkness. It was a good thing the bulb above the stairs was still in working order. "Don't go saying shit like that to Detective Kendrick. Next thing you know, I'll be bailing your ass out of jail."

Lance unfolded his large frame while flipping Noah the bird before heading back up to the kitchen.

"You can't tell me you didn't think of that. Hell, Mitch used to read those Stephen King and Dean Koontz novels like we used to skim through Uncle Jimmy's *Playboy* magazines. I might have borrowed a couple of books after Mitch went to boot camp. Anything you need to know about getting rid of bodies are somewhere in those pages."

Lance thought it in poor taste to recommend the body not be buried in a pet cemetery, though that type of dark humor had gotten him through some of the worst of times. Being pinned down with his unit outside of Kandahar during a road march came to mind. He'd come to rely on that black humor more times than he'd care to admit.

"Kendrick is the detective on the case," Noah pointed out, following Lance into the kitchen before he turned off the stairwell light and closed the basement door. "Why don't we leave the professionals to do their jobs, and we'll focus on our own business."

"Speaking of which, have you decided what you're going to do once you settle into your new digs?" Lance had no doubt what his intentions were, but Noah had never expressed interest in working with their dad. "There's not a lot of engineering jobs in Blyth Lake."

"No, there's not." Noah leaned against the far countertop and crossed his arms as if they had all the time in the world. A glance at Lance's phone told him that they had less than ten minutes to drive into town. "I haven't told Dad this, but I'm thinking of approaching Miles and Chad to join in their small business. Maybe I could handle the business and electrical installations end while they work the repair trucks. Let's face it. Wes and Clayton leaving the family business has definitely put Schaeffer's Contracting and Flooring into a bit of bind. Miles has been hiring outside electrical contractors for a few years. It would make sense for him to partner up with one full time."

"You could always freelance yourself, you know." Lance had always been a proponent of owning one's own business. "It would give you the ability to pick and choose your own jobs.

You certainly have the experience from your time in the Marines. Picking up your contracting license and your journeyman's certificate would be a cakewalk."

"I know, but I'd rather take some time and get used to being back in civilian life before I start my own shop."

Noah didn't have to explain his sentiment. It wasn't easy to go from such a regimented routine and people who would lay down their lives for you to people who could care less about honor and integrity.

Admittedly, the people of Blyth Lake would be a lot less of a challenge in that category than an everyday civilian. Most of the residents who lived in their small hometown were honest, trustworthy folks.

Of course, then there was the homicidal nut job running around that had everyone on edge.

"I don't think getting caught up in a twelve-year-old homicide investigation is what you had in mind, though." Lance pulled his keys from the front pocket of his jeans. "And I'm getting the feeling that you and Detective Kendrick don't think Sophia's murder was an isolated incident."

Noah raised an eyebrow, as if he was daring Lance to argue with that supposition.

"You do understand what you're suggesting with that assumption, don't you?"

"Yeah, I do," Noah replied softly, resting a hand on Lance's shoulder as they both headed for the door. "We just might have a bona fide serial killer roaming Blyth Lake."

CHAPTER FIVE

"**S**O I HEAR tell you went toe to toe with that harlot from Channel Five News."

Brynn wasn't startled by Rose's appearance in the least. The clanking of her bracelets gave her away long before she entered the small office of the bar located in the back near the restrooms. She was a sight for sore eyes, though.

"Please tell me that's a club sandwich from Annie's Diner," Brynn practically begged, holding her arms out while wiggling her fingers in anticipation. She didn't even address Rose's response to the confrontation that occurred last night. There was something to be said for loyalty, and Rose would always have her back. "I—"

"Skipped lunch, I know," Rose interrupted wryly, pulling back the white Styrofoam container before Brynn could take it out of her hands. "You better take care of yourself or I'm going to start thinking it was a mistake to let Tiny sell you this gin mill, missy."

"Don't get me wrong," Brynn warned, finally managing to snag the food from Rose's grip. She opened the top and inhaled the delicious aroma of chicken and bacon, humming in appreciation. "I'm not complaining in the least that this past month has been busy with all the attention this town is getting, but we certainly didn't start this month with the inventory to keep up with the demand."

Had it been anyone else besides Rose—well, that included Tiny, too—she would have had to clarify her statement. Brynn would have given anything for that young girl's body not to have been found in such a horrible manner. It was also wrong of her to be somewhat relieved it hadn't been Emma.

"You could have asked Tiny to help you out," Rose pointed out knowingly, taking a seat in the lone guest chair that had always been positioned in front of the desk for as long as Brynn could remember. "He was free today."

"No, he wasn't." Brynn pointed a steak fry in Rose's direction. "I know he had a meeting with Wes and Clayton Schaeffer regarding those additional cottages you want to add up at the lake. You, madam, are gilding the lily."

Brynn rolled her chair over to the small refrigerator in the corner, also a staple from years past, and grabbed a can of Classic Coke. She'd already popped the top before positioning herself back behind her desk.

"By the way, you shouldn't be meddling in the Schaeffer's business like that." Brynn held up her hand to stop Rose from coming up with excuses as to why she always felt the need to fix everyone's problems. "Wes and Clayton left the family business for their own reasons. Nothing you say on their behalf to Miles or Chad will ever make that okay in their eyes."

"I was ultimately hoping to get Wes and Clayton to realize how much they miss Blyth Lake and return home with their hats in their hands," Rose responded defensively, pulling a purple floral fan out from her purse. She opened the thin folded paper with a flick of her wrist. "Don't give me that look, young lady. It's the God's honest truth."

Brynn couldn't help but smile around the bite of food in her mouth upon hearing Rose chastise her the way she used to back in the day when she'd caught Rose spinning tales.

"What are you thinking of doing with the rental over by Noah Kendall's place?" Brynn asked, having meant to have broached this subject before. "Are you keeping it or do you plan to sell it outright?"

Brynn pointed another fry in Rose's direction, hoping to avoid another lecture about how Tiny would have signed over the bar for a dollar had Brynn allowed that to take place. Well, she hadn't gone to college to earn a business degree for nothing. She was still paying off her student debt, but the local bank had given her a small business loan in order to buy out the bar in full. She wouldn't have had it any other way. People from around these parts didn't cotton to being in someone's debt, and that included family.

"Don't misunderstand me, I love the apartment over the bar. But that would be better utilized as a small banquet hall for private parties and such, once I get it redesigned." Brynn had moved in upstairs to the spacious wide-open studio apartment after graduating college. It suited her needs, especially given the amount of time she'd been spending in the office sorting out the financials and planning for additional growth. "But now that I've got a handle on things, I was thinking it would be nice to have somewhere away from the noise and the smell of stale beer."

"If I told you that you could move in tomorrow for a dollar, I don't suppose you'd do that, now would you?"

Brynn laughed, having had this same discussion with Tiny at the beginning of summer.

"Just think about it," Brynn said softly, wishing Rose and Tiny wouldn't worry about her so much. On the other hand, it was nice to know someone loved her as much as she loved them. "As for that reporter you asked about, let's just say she needed to be made aware of certain boundaries. Her upbringing in the city left her a bit unprepared for the rigors of country life."

Rose's laughter flittered through the small office, causing Brynn to breathe a little easier. She would never do anything to tarnish the name of Tiny's Cavern nor disappoint the Phifers in any way.

"Rose, do you think Blyth Lake has a serial killer in its midst?" Brynn had suddenly lost her appetite, but she didn't want Rose to know that. She played with the toothpick that had held her sandwich together as she waited for an answer. "Do you reckon that's what happened to Emma?"

"I've felt the change in the air, as well," Rose said with an uneasy sigh and a shake of her head. "I don't want to believe anyone we know could be capable of something so damn evil, but I was there the day Noah and Reese called the police. You should have seen the people lining up on the road that day, looking at each other with suspicion. It broke my heart."

Brynn noticed that Rose didn't answer the question.

Was Sophia's murder linked to Emma's disappearance?

Word throughout town had spread rather quickly after the state police had gotten involved. It was all the gossip mill could churn out, even here at the bar.

"Honey, do you remember something?" Rose asked, tilting her head to the side so that one of her earrings dangled lower than the other. "Did something happen to jog your memory?"

"Unfortunately, no." Bryn gave up the pretense of eating the rest of her dinner and pushed away the Styrofoam container. "I just can't help but think Emma suffered a horrible death at the hands of some monster. I overheard one of the camera guys on Charlene Weston's crew say that the police were finally going to reveal the autopsy report sometime real soon."

Rose held up her fan as if defending herself against the horrific details. For some reason, Brynn couldn't help but wonder how bad Sophia had suffered in her last final hours. Some of the townsfolk were in denial, saying that Sophia's death must have been some kind of freak accident and that it was in no way related to Emma's disappearance.

Brynn was on the other side of the camp with those residents who firmly believed someone in Blyth Lake walked among them with a shadow for a soul. She just wanted to be proven wrong.

"You know what?" Brynn said, pushing back her chair and grabbing her soda. "Let's head back up front to check on Kristen. This is the first afternoon I've left her to handle the bar alone. I'm sure she's at her wits' end by now."

"She had everything under control when I walked through." Rose nodded her approval as she tucked her purple fan back into her lavender-colored purse. It wasn't a brand name, though most people in Blyth Lake shopped either at the small boutique on Main Street or drove the twenty miles outside the town's limits to either a Walmart or Target in the city. "You made a good hire in that one, Brynn."

"I heard about Mindy quitting on you up at the lake's restaurant." Brynn had come very close to being the one to give Mindy a job, but she was always on her phone and in everyone's business. That wouldn't have gone over well in an establishment where alcohol loosened lips. "Tiny said you had some interviews lined up for next Monday. Does that mean you're going to have to play hostess this weekend?"

"Goodness, no!" Rose exclaimed with an enchanting but wicked laugh. Oh, that meant she was up to one of her tricks that had everyone scrambling to be far away when she pulled the trigger. "Tiny and I had a small wager rather than risk it to chance, and I happened to win it this very morning."

Brynn covered one ear with the soda can and the other with

her hand as she walked out of her office. She could still here Rose chuckling, but it at least stopped her from sharing whatever playfulness she and Tiny had partaken with each other in the bedroom.

"...that detective. Nothing came of it, so now the media is waiting for the autopsy report."

"...heard that Lance got the Fetter place. I'm glad he's cleared up things with the police."

"...saw Reese at the school. I wouldn't be surprised to see a ring on her finger, though their relationship moved a little fast for my liking, if you know what I mean."

Brynn wished she'd kept her ears covered as she made her way to the bar. The place had become busier over the last few hours, and it appeared everyone was still talking about the Kendalls and the body being found in one of their homes. She doubted it would change much over the course of the next few weeks, but she could always hope talk switched to sports. Fantasy Football was about to begin, and that was a pretty big deal around here.

"How are things going out here, Kristen?"

Brynn couldn't have asked for more as she looked behind the counter to see all the used glasses had been washed and put in their respective places, along with everyone's drink topped off on the bar.

Satisfaction washed over her at the knowledge that at least one of her new hires was working out. Tiny had taken on many roles here, cutting out the need to hire more than three people at a time—a waitress who handled the tables during the evening crowd rush, a fry cook who pretty much stuck to making wings and burgers, and Brynn.

She'd done whatever was needed at the time.

Rose and Tiny were getting to the point where they'd rather

have a few nights off here and there, so they were now investing in real estate near the lake. Their property up on the water had brought them the most revenue in the past, and this way they could delegate while freeing up more time for them to enjoy their own lives in early retirement, of sorts.

Well, that had been the goal. Everyone knew they were too invested in the local community to travel the world, but a couple weeks twice a year was manageable.

"I've got things covered, boss."

Brynn winced at the title, but she let it slide. Kristen was overzealous at times, but she was downright one of the best bartenders this side of Cleveland. She had short hair that framed her face, the red color definitely from a bottle, and she wore her makeup like a shield. One of her arms was covered in tattoos and her right ear had multiple piercings. She might have an outer shell that was used as a barrier, but there was a vulnerable side she'd hidden rather well. Only an expert could see things for what they were.

There was a reason Kristen wanted to leave the city. She'd been upfront, though the truth had been somewhat vague. Something in the girl's green eyes told Brynn she'd needed this gig and a chance to start over.

Brynn understood all too well about new beginnings.

"Honey, I'm going to drive over to the lake to see how things are coming along with the cottages." Rose grabbed a bag of Tiny's favorite chips before telling everyone goodbye. "I'll see you late tonight. Put these on my tab."

"That's going on your tab for real," Brynn called out, getting a rise out of the usuals at the bar. "We're starting you one today."

A ball cap that she hadn't seen in a while caught her attention.

Jimmy Webb. He was Lance's uncle, though he was estranged from the Kendall clan. Doing a stint in prison and not being the most upstanding guy had a way of doing that. He'd stained the family name and most folks didn't appreciate that around here.

The man also claimed to be the last one to see Emma Irwin alive. He'd told the police he saw Emma walking down Seventh Street the night she disappeared.

Brynn hadn't meant to stare at Jimmy for so long and was startled when his striking blue eyes met hers, almost as if to tell her that he could hear her thoughts.

Brynn quickly looked away, wondering if there was more to his story than he let on. It was then she realized that she was doing exactly what she'd accused the other townsfolk of earlier—regarding those she'd known her whole life with unfounded suspicion.

CHAPTER SIX

"LANCE, JUST LET me talk to Dad," Gwen requested irritably, paper rustling in the background of their phone connection. What was she doing working this late on a Thursday evening? "I was hoping he'd stop by the new storefront and measure my office."

"He's, uh…" Lance could have kicked himself. What had possessed him to let Gwen think he was at the family homestead? He hadn't wanted her to know he was at his new place, that's why. He had no choice but to make up a story. Besides, he was the youngest, so his father should have known he wasn't good at keeping secrets. "With Noah."

"Yeah, isn't that crazy that he found a body in the wall of his house?" Gwen must be really distracted if she hadn't caught the hesitation in Lance's tone. "It's horrible when you think about it."

"Yeah, you didn't know Sophia Morton like I did. She attended summer camp together the year Emma went missing."

"And the authorities think there's a connection? What the heck is going on back there?"

"I would be surprised if there wasn't a correlation," Lance admitted, quietly closing the self-winding metal measuring tape so that Gwen didn't hear the sound. "It's too much of a coincidence not to be connected in some way."

"I still can't get over the fact that Noah would buy up the

old Yoder farmhouse the minute he got home. It must have been the fastest closing in county history." Gwen was hitting a little too close to home, and Lance needed to figure out a way to change the subject. "Noah doesn't even know what he wants to do with his future, so how can he be so sure he can afford the payments on that kind of mortgage? The property associated with that farm has got to be at least twenty acres. It was a dairy farm, once upon a time."

Leave it to Gwen to be the practical one.

"Noah mentioned to me this morning that he's thinking of approaching Miles Schaeffer for an electrician job, maybe talking to them about a partnership and taking on the management responsibilities while they handle the trucks, doing repair calls and such."

Lance had spent the last hour taking measurements of each room in his new home, saving the basement for last. He hadn't been ready to call it a night when he and his dad had left Noah's place. The renovations his brother had done over the course of the last couple of months had been simply astounding. It spurred Lance's desire to get started on his own repairs. He wanted to make something of what he'd been given, as well.

"Really? That would work. Have you seen what electricians are making these days? Trade jobs are going unfulfilled, so the demand is relatively high for skilled labor."

"Hey, sis, I have another call coming through," Lance said with a wince. He'd be mincemeat if Gwen caught on to him making up excuses and the secret got out. "I'll have Dad give you a call tomorrow."

Three seconds later, Lance disconnected the call and shoved his phone inside the front pocket of his jeans. It would make his life a hell of a lot easier if the rest of his siblings followed suit and came back home already. Jace was supposed to be here in a few weeks, while Gwen wasn't due home until sometime in September. Maybe he would just avoid her calls for a while to make things easier for himself.

Leave it to Mitch to come home twelve years to the month from the time Emma Irwin disappeared. Hell, if the town thought the Kendall siblings had anything to do with murder or kidnapping before, the timing of their homecoming certainly wasn't helping things. All that the local townsfolk needed to start wagging their tongues was a coincidence or two to encourage the gristmill to churn out a few tall tales.

Lance reached for the dangling string that had once been white with every intention of turning off the bulb so that he could return upstairs until something caught his eye. The metal access door to the HVAC squirrel cage was slightly skewed. Whoever had changed the filter last must not have secured the quarter-turn twist latches properly. It would only take a second to make sure the filter was good to go and slip the panel back in place.

Lance sighed in resignation, knowing it would drive him crazy if he didn't take care of it now. Thankfully, his father had the utilities turned on the day before Lance arrived into town. Lance had fired up the pilot lights on the gas appliances that still required them, and he also checked the meter for an initial usage reading. What little light there was from the lone bulb gave off enough brightness for him to see what he was doing.

He hooked the tape measure to his belt before turning the latch thumbscrews to disengage them and removing the thin sheet of metal. He might as well make sure there wasn't something in the track of the access door while he was down here, and he needed to determine the filter size so that he could get replacements.

People never changed these damn things as often as they

should. A monthly change on an older house like this one wasn't beyond reason, especially since he was going to be kicking up dust with all his repairs. He was even thinking it might be a good idea to get all the vents swept out professionally to get things started on the right track and to see if they had any mold or excessive dust in them. Furnace filters would be one of the many things he could add to his list for tomorrow's run to the hardware store.

"What the hell…"

There was a small tin box lying on its side with one of those magnets attached to it, almost as if it had fallen from somewhere inside the unit. Lance leaned the metal panel against the wall before kneeling to get a better look at what had come loose from inside the ductwork. It was larger than an Altoids container. It kind of looked like an old Velvet Pipe and Cigarette Tobacco tin.

Lance hadn't seen one of those around going on ten years or more, so it wouldn't be much of a surprise to find out the heater needed to be replaced due to its age and infrequent periodic maintenance.

He picked up what he thought would be some discarded tobacco container. It was far from something that belonged inside the furnace's ductwork.

Lance shifted his weight so that he could shed more light on the object in his hand. It reminded him of his grandfather's habit of smoking a pipe when he would come over for Sunday dinner. Of course, Mary Kendall never allowed her father to smoke his old Velvet tobacco inside her house.

Lance shook the tin to find that something was still inside, though he doubted it was tobacco from the weight of it. He carefully pried opened the lid, hoping like hell it wasn't some dead carcass. Old man Fetter was known for making odd contraptions, and it wouldn't surprise Lance if this was some kind of rigged mousetrap of some sort.

"Huh."

Polaroid pictures.

Who the hell used Polaroid pictures anymore?

The photographs appeared faded with age, but it was hard to tell what the subject was with the limited lighting. He began to put the top back on the tin when he abruptly stopped mid-motion.

There was absolutely no way in hell was he looking at a picture of Emma Irwin.

A sick feeling set up shop in his stomach. What were the odds of him finding photographs in his new home after his brother had discovered a body in the drywall of his house? This had to be somebody's idea of a sick joke. Would his brother take a prank this far just to spook him?

Lance tilted the box to show himself that he'd been mistaken, but Emma's long brunette hair was easy to recognize.

"Son of a bitch."

Lance replaced the cover and then quickly stood, seating the metal covering in the slats so that the ductwork was secure and the filter was in place. It wasn't long before he'd cast the basement into darkness, taking the basement stairs to the kitchen two at a time. He'd already taken his cell phone out to make a call to the sheriff's department when he thought better of it.

Noah and their father had explained how Sheriff Percy was in the process of being removed from office, causing quite a stir among the longtime residents. It would be better to contact Detective Kendrick with what Lance had found, though he couldn't imagine it had anything to do with Emma Irwin's disappearance. Those pictures had been there for a very long time from the looks of things. It couldn't be his brother fooling around with him.

Lance forced himself to stop at the small kitchen counter and set the tin box down on the laminate surface. There had to be a reasonable explanation as to why these photographs were hidden in the old Fetter house.

Arthur Fetter had lived in Blyth Lake since the day he'd been born, so it wasn't a stretch that he and his family had known the Irwins. *Right?* Maybe the man's grandson or granddaughter had stored the pictures in a vent up in one of the bedrooms. They might have stored them away as mementos for when they visited their grandfather in the summers.

It was a plausible explanation, but Lance couldn't bring himself to believe the rationalization he'd snatched out of midair.

"Open it," Lance urged himself, his thoughts automatically contradicting that idea due to fingerprints. He could already hear Noah's response to that excuse, especially considering his reaction to the cemetery idea. Was he overreacting? Honestly, the cemetery idea had some relevance if what he thought was in the box was really inside the tin can. "Shit."

Lance's fingerprints were already covering the outside of the evidence, so it wouldn't matter if he took another look to verify his suspicions. It could very well be souvenirs one of the Fetter family members had kept as a token, but there was only one way to find out. And he certainly didn't want to call Noah or Detective Kendrick if this turned out to be a harmless keepsake. Hell, it might not even be Emma. It might be another girl with the same style of hair.

The tin cover hit the counter with a shrill ting, revealing Emma Irwin's smile sure as the day he'd last seen her.

Lance lifted the picture away from the small stack, his chest becoming painful when his gaze landed on the next photograph.

Sophia Morton.

Holy shit.

He stared in disbelief at the girl whose body had been found in his brother's house.

His conscious mind was telling him that he'd discovered photographs of victims—seven girls were counted after he'd set each Polaroid on the counter—but he was still in denial. Besides, there was one photograph of a teenager who he knew one hundred percent to be alive. There had to be a reasonable explanation as to why these pictures were in this box inside the heating unit of a house that had been sitting empty for the last nine months.

Lance couldn't come up with one plausible explanation.

He'd set his phone on the counter before taking the lid off the tin can, so he picked it up with an unsteady hand and speed-dialed his brother before he could formulate the words that might come out of his mouth.

He was still staring in horror at the photographs, but in particular Emma and Sophia, when Noah finally answered on the fifth ring.

"Hello?"

"Noah, you need to call Detective Kendrick and get him over to my place as fast as you can." Lance swallowed the painful lump in his throat as he finally uttered what had been thrashing around in his head. "I think Arthur Fetter murdered Sophia Morton, as well as Emma Irwin and a bunch of other girls. You better get that detective's ass moving, like, right now."

CHAPTER SEVEN

"**J**EREMY, I THINK it's time you call it a night."

Brynn swept her gaze across the empty tables, double checking that she hadn't missed wiping one down after the majority of the crowd had slowly dissipated. It was going on one-forty-five in the morning, leaving only fifteen minutes before she closed the doors. Last call had been a half an hour ago, and Jeremy was still nursing his last drink. She'd let Kristen go a couple of hours ago, already owing her overtime for coming in early to try out a shift on her own.

The night had gone better than expected, allowing Brynn more time to cater toward her clientele. She truly wanted to know what would make the Cavern better in terms of service and a place to spend an evening rather than heading into the city. It would take some remodeling, but the full kitchen would allow for food other than short order items to be served for special occasions.

Everyone had been unanimous in having a live band on the weekends, as well as adding more pool tables and televisions to live-stream more than two teams on any given Sunday.

It didn't surprise Brynn that Jeremy Bell was the last to leave. It had always been like that ever since she was a teenager. Jeremy was what bar owners called a regular.

"Is Whitney picking you up?" Brynn asked, trying to gauge how Jeremy was doing. She had maintained tabs on exactly how much he'd had to drink this evening, but his tolerance depended on more than one variable. It was highly unusual to see him nursing his drink. Maybe Doctor Finley had finally been able to talk some sense into the man. "I can look outside to see if her car is in the lot."

"She ain't here. She's out of town for the week." Jeremy didn't sound too disappointed at that little fact. "Whitney is with that scumbag she's been dating. What she sees in him is beyond me. Wasting her time is what she's doin'."

Brynn wasn't about to disagree with Jeremy. His daughter hadn't been known to have the best choice in men, with the exception of Noah Kendall back in the day. Since then, it had been one bad pick after another.

"I'm sure he'll show his true colors sooner or later," Brynn replied, wanting to give Jeremy hope. He wasn't that bad of a guy, though he certainly didn't wear a halo. "I can give you a ride home, if you like."

"I truly appreciate that, Brynn." Jeremy pushed his bottle of beer toward her before he stood from the stool he'd been sitting on for the past eight hours. She didn't bother to ask him to pay his tab when he would settle up come Sunday. He and Tiny had agreed to that little arrangement years ago, and she wouldn't break that tradition. "But I think some air will do me good. Before you know it, winter will be here and walking will be out of the picture."

"Oh, don't go skipping the rest of autumn. That's my favorite season, you know." Brynn swiped the bottle from the wooden countertop and poured the rest of the contents down the drain before tossing the dark brown glass bottle into the recycling bin. "There's something about the change of color in the leaves that seems very peaceful."

Jeremy muttered something about the fall season being anything but peaceful, but she must have misunderstood. He was out the door before she could ask him to repeat what he'd said, which was for the best. She was exhausted from doing so much paperwork and setting up additional interviews for the two waitress positions she'd decided to add on to her payroll.

Brynn began pulling out the plastic bag from the garbage can underneath the bar, drawing the strings together so that it would be easier to remove it from the large container. She decided to leave the bag until last, choosing to wipe down the wooden surface of the counter so that she could head upstairs to her apartment after dumping the garbage into the dumpster out back.

"What did you forget, Jeremy?" Brynn called out after hearing the front door open with a whoosh. The wind must be picking up, which meant a storm was brewing from the west. "Did you change your mind about that—"

Brynn shut her mouth with a snap of her teeth.

She'd expected to see Lance Kendall at some point, but his presence at this very moment was like a physical blow to her heart.

All the Kendall brothers resembled one another, but there had always been something special about Lance that touched her soul. It had nothing to do with his jet-black hair, startling blue eyes, and chiseled features. It also had nothing to do with his broad chest and muscular body, though that certainly didn't take points away from his appeal.

No.

Lance Kendall was different than any other man Brynn had ever met, and that included her time away at college. He was the only one who ever truly understood who she was as a woman...the good and the bad of all that she was.

"Brynn, it's good to see you."

She hadn't realized that she'd stopped wiping the bar and was staring in his direction with her lips slightly parted in surprise, but she quickly rectified her posture and allowed her usual barrier to slip into place. Life had come between them, and that was no one's fault…but that didn't mean the leftover pain didn't still throb every now and then.

"Lance," Brynn greeted him once she'd found her voice, tossing the wet rag into the sink before she made a conscious decision to meet him halfway. It would have been rude to do otherwise. "It's good to see you, too."

Growing up in a small town made things easier in the long run. Everyone knew everyone else, comfort and support were part of the package, and friendly hugs given as greetings. A neighbor was part of an extended family, and they all took care of their own. There were times, though, that type of familiarity was an obstacle…like now.

She still couldn't bring herself to take that last step.

Worse, she stopped breathing when he did it for her.

Home.

She could have sworn she'd heard someone whisper the lone word into her ear, but she'd had to close her eyes when his warmth enveloped her. The sense of security he'd given her throughout her high school years returned out of nowhere. It wasn't until now that she realized just how much she'd missed him. He'd been her best friend, her first lover, and yes…her soulmate for as long as she could remember.

Brynn tried to steel herself against the heartache that was bound to return, but instead, her arms instinctively wrapped around his neck and held tight. She now wanted to capture this moment for all eternity, because this wasn't real. He was a long-lost friend she hadn't seen in a while. That was all.

She understood this brief flash of make-believe would dissipate the second his arms dropped from her waist.

She didn't care, though.

She could be selfish just this once.

Brynn inhaled deeply, wondering how it was that a man could still smell the same after all these years. Flashes of him wearing a suit to their homecoming dance flittered through her mind. His intoxicating scent of rich cedar wood and warm ginger melted her soul as it struggled to remain intact and ward off the thousands of memories bombarding her psyche.

"God, I've missed you," Lance said with a harsh honesty that almost had her believing he'd actually come back for her.

Her heart ached just a little more at his words.

Brynn squeezed her eyes tight in an attempt to break this spell he'd cast over her with just a simple embrace. She was quite proud of herself when she loosened her hold on him, took a step back, and managed to meet his genuine gaze of longing.

"Welcome home," Brynn said softly, though she was sincere with every word. She even achieved a matching smile. He'd made it home alive, and that was saying something. How many times had she watched the news regarding servicemen and women not returning home to their loved ones? "Your dad has talked about nothing else since…"

Brynn winced when she realized where her train of thought had taken her. Mary Kendall died three years ago after a hard-fought battle against cancer. Everyone was well aware that her final wish was to have all her children back in Blyth Lake, raising their families together in a small town setting where family meant everything. Brynn hadn't meant to bring up painful memories.

"You wouldn't be willing to extend your business hours, would you?"

It could have been the way Lance had slanted his request, or it could have been the slight desperation she'd caught in his blue eyes, but her innate need to sooth his troubles won out over common sense.

Would anyone else have caught the slight tension in the lines around his eyes?

Even after all these years, she was still able to read him like a book. Which meant he could do the same with her. She would do well to remember that in the future.

"I can do one better." Brynn brushed past him and walked to the front entrance where she turned off the neon sign and flipped the deadbolt. She would secure all the locks once he'd left after one drink. "What can I get you? My treat."

"A shot of anything strong enough that will make what I just saw fade into oblivion."

Brynn would have stumbled at his almost desperate declaration had she not been expecting something dire from the tension radiating off his body. Instead, she managed to gracefully make her way behind the bar where she grabbed a bottle of her best blended Canadian whiskey. Tiny always told her that nothing soothed a soul like a glass of Crown Royal XR, created from the last few barrels produced by the famous LaSalle distillery.

"Is this about the investigation into Sophia Morton's death?" Brynn poured two fingers worth of the golden liquor into two glasses before pushing one his way. She was proud of herself that there wasn't a tremor to be found in her hand. "Has something else happened?"

"You might say that." Lance nodded toward the drink in front of him. "Thank you."

Lance took a seat on one of the bar stools and slid his glass closer. He then lifted the tumbler and twirled the liquid around before taking a healthy drink. She wasn't surprised when he tilted his head to the side with an easy smile as the smooth whiskey slid down his throat.

"I'll be honest with you, Brynn. I thought we knew everyone in this town…what they stood for, what morals they embodied, and what they were capable of doing. Now? It's like I'm still out there on the battlefield, not knowing who to trust besides those who I've brought with me."

Lance didn't need to explain who those people were—his family.

Other than that?

Something bad must have happened for him to question everyone else in this town. Then again, hadn't she been doing the very same thing just this afternoon?

"What happened?" It was rare that Brynn ever sat behind the bar, but she did keep a tall stool tucked underneath the counter for when it was needed. She hauled it out and took a seat, instinctively knowing she was going to want it for the support. "You've only been home a couple of days. Don't tell me you found a body, too."

She wasn't surprised when Lance's right eyebrow rose in question, almost as if he were asking her why she hadn't been by to say hello. Well, that worked both ways. Plus, she didn't doubt that he would eventually make his way here—Tiny's Cavern was pretty much all the nightlife Blyth Lake had to offer on any given weeknight or weekend.

Brynn joked with him about finding a body in his house like his brother, but she couldn't bring herself to believe something that serious had happened again. They'd both known Sophia, even though it had only been a brief moment in time. And Brynn couldn't even think of Emma without a painful slice to her heart. Had she been discarded in such a senseless manner also?

No, this wasn't the time to use laughter as a way to alleviate the fear. Her jest had been inappropriate.

"I think Arthur Fetter might be responsible for Sophia's death."

It was a good thing she hadn't been holding her own glass. It was currently secure on the counter, but not for long. The contents inside would give her the stability she needed to handle such accusations.

Besides, Brynn had to have heard Lance wrong, because Arthur Fetter was one of the nicest men she'd ever met. As a matter of fact, he'd sent her a care package or two back when she'd been in college. He was like an honorary grandfather to those around town who didn't have one left.

"I'm sorry," Brynn said with a shake of her head and a disbelieving laugh, indicating how preposterous that idea sounded. Unfortunately, Lance didn't join in on the joke. "I thought you said Arthur was responsible for Sophia's murder, but both you and I know that can't be right."

"Oh, I said Arthur Fetter, alright. I also think that whatever he did to Sophia, he did the same to Emma and numerous other teenage girls." Lance appeared as if he wanted to throw up the contents he'd just downed, but he pressed his hand hard against his mouth. She was honestly speechless. They both picked up their glasses in unison and took another drink. "I found pictures in my basement of seven young women—one murdered, one missing, and it doesn't take a genius to figure out what happened to the others. My basement, Brynn. The house my parents bought me. I just can't wrap my head around the idea of this."

Lance drained the last of his whiskey, slamming the glass down and indicating he wanted another by waving her in. She wasn't about to deny him this little bit of comfort. She also tried to come up with a reasonable excuse as to why photographs of teenage girls would be in the basement of Arthur's old house, but she was coming up blank.

"There's more."

Lance's declaration had Brynn refilling her own glass of whiskey. She set the bottle down with a thud and braced herself for another blow.

"I saw Arthur walking down Seventh Street the night I snuck Sophia and Emma out of camp that summer. I think that's when he saw those girls and started to plan their murders."

CHAPTER EIGHT

LANCE HAD BEEN dealing with Detective Kendrick and his cronies for the last four hours. He'd had a forensics team come in and search the house from top to bottom, unable to find anything else that might give them more understanding as to why a metal tin with keepsake photographs had been hidden inside the furnace or the ductwork of the HVAC system.

Every minute that passed had spawned more questions for both of them.

And they were still ratcheting up in numbers.

This was the first time since he'd made the shocking discovery that he experienced some semblance of balance. Brynn always had been able to stabilize his emotions with a mere look of reassurance. She'd been his rock throughout his junior and senior years, even seeming to understand his need to graduate early and enlist in the Marines.

That life-changing decision had been hard on both of them, but for Lance it had been a foregone conclusion. He would have given anything had Brynn decided to join him after boot camp, but he'd understood her reasoning for staying behind with her adopted family.

Blyth Lake was her home, after all.

It wouldn't have been fair to take her away from the only people she'd called family just to follow him around from one duty station to another. Lance had seen how hard deployments had been on his fellow Marines' relationships. The Corps was very tough on the entire family as a general rule.

Yet this was still where he'd found himself compelled to go when he needed a bit of sanity after the discovery he'd made this evening.

"You saw Arthur walking down Seventh Street the night Sophia went to talk to Ms. Osburn?"

"In my defense, I never asked why Sophia and Emma wanted me to drive them into town that night. I was doing them a favor in return for another." The subtle quality of the premium whiskey had definitely entered his bloodstream, reducing his inhibitions. Some of the shock from earlier was starting to wear off and the warm liquor was chasing away the cobwebs while lubricating his tongue. "If you remember correctly, Sophia promised she'd stand guard while we went for a certain swim later that night."

A slight flush of color began to cover Brynn's cheeks at the recollection, though it could have easily been due to the whiskey as well. There was something he wanted to say before they started to dissect past events.

"Brynn, I never did tell you how much it meant to me that you kept in touch that first year I was deployed. Your friendship…well, I didn't take it for granted. It was hard when we grew apart and you stopped writing."

Lance selfishly looked over her features, noting the slight differences between then and now. She had the most flawless skin he'd ever seen on a woman, and that hadn't changed one bit. Her light coloring matched her blonde hair, which was currently pulled back at the nape of her neck. It was easy to see that she hadn't touched the length, leaving it to fall just below her shoulders as she always had.

Her brown eyes used to remind him of those creamy, soft

caramel candies the grocery store carried around Halloween time. It was also the ones his mother used to make those caramel apples that he loved so much. Brynn's irises were still fawn colored, and damned if they still didn't make a piece of him melt in her presence.

"Lance, there's no denying that what we had back then was special for the both of us." Brynn shifted in unease on the stool she was sitting on behind the bar, as if she would rather be discussing Arthur Fetter and the possibility that he was a serial killer. She always was a woman to face things head on, and now was no different. "Our decisions...we didn't make them out of spite or in haste. We both chose our paths long before we hit our senior year. Bitterness doesn't have a place between the two of us."

Brynn appeared to hesitate briefly before she downed the rest of the contents in her glass. She leaned to the side and set the empty tumbler inside the sink. He was honestly surprised when she settled back into place and continued with the original topic of discussion. He thought maybe his time here had come to an end.

"Did you see Arthur's car anywhere near where you parked your truck that night?"

Lance thought back to when Sophia and Emma had gotten out of his truck to walk in the direction of Main Street. He'd stayed behind and listened to music on the radio, not really concerned that someone would see his vehicle on that end of town. It was the reason he'd chosen that area to park to begin with, which was why he hadn't paid much attention to any of the other vehicles on the street.

"I had other things on my mind back then," Lance said honestly with a raised eyebrow. Another flush decorated her cheeks, but that didn't stop her from explaining why she'd asked about Arthur's car.

"He used to regularly visit his wife's gravesite at the cemetery. Maybe he was either walking toward or away from there when you saw him."

Brynn tucked that one loose lock of hair he'd been wanting to rub between his fingers behind her ear. She didn't have to explain how she'd known that tidbit of information, because Lance used to accompany her on the weekends to the cemetery so that she could spend time at her parents' graves.

Seriously, had there been anything they hadn't known about each other back then?

"Arthur made a point to go to the graveyard on Sunday morning," Lance gently reminded her, not needing to point out that a Tuesday evening was a far cry from the end of the week. At least, he thought he'd snuck the girls out on a Tuesday evening. It could have been Wednesday, but the same principle applied. "It doesn't matter, Brynn. Detective Kendrick had a forensics team go through the house with a fine-tooth comb. While they didn't find any evidence that he committed murder inside his home, that doesn't mean—"

Brynn held up her hand before Lance could finish his sentence. She didn't want to hear that Sophia had been murdered in Arthur Fetter's house, because that could very possibly mean he'd done the same thing to Emma.

"I refuse to believe gentle-souled Arthur Fetter had anything to do with what happened to either Sophia or Emma."

"You know, I was talking to Noah this morning about the cemetery being a good place to hide a body. It doesn't seem so farfetched now, especially after I saw Fetter that night." Lance lifted the glass to his lips and drained the rest of his whiskey without a flutter of his eye after having gotten used to the satisfying burn. He thought about having another, but he still needed to drive home. Well, to his father's house, anyway. "Kendrick let me know that forensics didn't find any blood in the house, but I'll be staying with my dad for the next couple of days till I get things together over at the house."

"That's probably for the best," Brynn agreed, resting both forearms on the wooden countertop. It was more than apparent she would wait for hardcore evidence before believing Arthur Fetter might very well be a serial killer. "Say you were right and Arthur did see Sophia and Emma that night. Why would he take Emma and then wait a year before targeting Sophia? It doesn't make sense if your theory was right about him."

"This is why we're not detectives." Lance wanted to make it very clear he didn't have any intentions of getting involved in the murder investigation any more than he already was, and the same went for Noah. "Detective Kendrick has the photographs now. Maybe he can pull some prints off the pictures or the tin can they were kept in to prove Arthur knew about their existence."

"Your fingerprints will be on the photographs as well." It was uncanny how similar the two of them viewed situations, and this proved to him that their connection hadn't been altered. She also proved that he wasn't crazy to assume those kinds of things. "And Noah *was* one of the people to find Sophia's body. Do you think—"

"Wait," Lance interrupted with a bit of disbelief. He was totally on board with the fingerprints, and he'd even added his two cents about the cemetery, but Brynn was taking this to a whole new level. "You think one of us could have—"

"God, no," Brynn protested, sitting up a little straighter as she defended her position. It was obvious he offended her for putting words into her mouth, but there had been an underlying accusation that he wasn't so comfortable with, especially after tonight's events. "No. That isn't what I meant at all. I was suggesting that maybe someone has a grudge against your family and is trying to implicate one or more of you in this crime. Come on. You can't tell me you don't find it odd that two out of the five houses your parents purchased end up containing physical evidence that points toward Blyth Lake having a serial killer."

Well, when she put it like that…

"But Sophia's body was sealed inside that wall eleven years ago. No one could have known who would end up discovering the body, if anyone did. The pictures I found tonight were taken at least twelve years ago, maybe even longer than that if Detective Kendrick can get positive identifications on the other girls in those photos." Lance couldn't see how that could be connected to the Kendalls. "Mitch, Jace, and Gwen weren't even in town back then. I can't see how any of this could have anything to do with us."

Brynn tossed out Jimmy Webb's name, but Lance automatically rejected that idea. His uncle might not be the most upstanding guy, but he wasn't a serial killer. To be quite honest, he wasn't smart enough to pull something like that off without leaving behind evidence.

"The simple fact is that being an asshole doesn't make one a murderer."

It was going on zero four hundred before Lance realized it, both of them coming up with numerous scenarios as to who had access to the Anderson farmhouse and the Fetter property. Except for the subject matter, it was the most relaxing conversation he'd had since signing his discharge papers. Then again, that could have had something to do with the whiskey they'd consumed.

"Have dinner with me tomorrow." Lance waited for Brynn

to either accept his invitation or try to find an excuse as to why that wouldn't be the best of ideas. Honestly, he thought it was a fantastic suggestion. He gently rested his hand on hers when it was obvious she was going to stand and push her stool back. "I've missed you for far too long, blondie."

Brynn pursed her lips to keep from smiling at the old nickname he'd given her back in high school. She'd gone through a phase of listening to the old rock band, and he'd caught her singing at the top of her lungs at one of the intersections in town. It was in that moment when she hadn't thought anyone was watching that he'd caught a glimpse of the carefree woman she was on the inside. That one hapless unguarded moment had captured the heart of a teenage boy.

There were times throughout the last twelve years that he wasn't sure he'd ever gotten his heart back, because he'd never been able to fully commit to any other woman. Then again, it might have had to do with the fact that he'd been deployed every so many months. Military life was certainly hard on relationships, let alone committed ones.

"We went our separate ways, Lance," Brynn said softly, though he could hear her regret. Still, she slowly pulled her hand from underneath his. "We can't change what was done."

"You'd be surprised at what could be changed if you want it bad enough."

Lance stood and reached for his wallet, but the narrowing of her caramel colored eyes had him rethinking his gesture.

"This was two old friends having a drink," Brynn said, tilting her head to one side as if she were sizing him up for some reason. "I'm not open for business."

She only ever looked at him like that when she was about to propose something that would no doubt get them in trouble. He held up a finger and tossed her words back at her good-naturedly, though he respectively disagreed with her belief.

"We can't change the past, as you said, so I'd rethink whatever it is you're about to suggest."

"Touché."

Lance waited a few more seconds, hoping that she would throw caution to the wind and propose whatever had been on her mind.

"Stubborn," Lance muttered with a shake of his head, her laugh ringing out over the bar as if it were Christmas. He hadn't realized how much he'd missed home until this very moment. What surprised him most was that he thought of her as home. "I have missed you, blondie. I can't help but wonder how much time we're both going to waste pretending we're just old friends."

Lance slapped the counter as a bid goodbye and then made his way toward the exit. He slowed his gait, hoping that she would change her mind about his invitation. The only sound he heard was running water, indicating that she was already washing away his presence.

He was confident her endeavor wouldn't be that easy, because he could already tell the night ahead would be a sleepless one...and it had nothing to do with Sophia Morton, Emma Irwin, or Arthur Fetter. He'd done his duty and handed over the evidence he'd found in his house. As far as he was concerned, his part in that particular nightmare was done. What lay in his path was the fact that he had his own troubles to deal with.

No, sleep wasn't in his foreseeable future, because he had no doubt that a certain blonde was all he'd see when he tried to close his eyes.

Brynn was right, in a funny kind of way.

Some things didn't change just because some small measure of time had passed.

CHAPTER NINE

"WHAT HAS YOU all worked up into a tizzy?"

Brynn blew away the flyaway strands blocking her view, well aware Julie Brigham was standing on the other side of the bar. It was still relatively early, so Jeremy Bell had yet to claim his seat at the counter.

Regardless of the early hour, there were a few customers who had shown up here for some wings and a beer instead of going over to Annie's Diner for lunch. Cassie Osburn, the daughter of the infamous Annie, had yet to go in front of a judge for her role in trying to scare Reese Woodward out of town.

Word had it that Sophia Morton had dug up some kind of compromising pictures of Annie Osburn from her time as an actress in California. Cassie had been afraid Reese's presence would dredge up history best left forgotten. She'd let the fear of her mother's disgrace push her into doing the wrong thing.

Needless to say, everyone wanted a view from the front row seats.

"I'm not in a *tizzy*," Brynn protested as she ripped open a box of cocktail napkins she'd gotten from the supply closet. The last thing she needed was for her friend to find out that Lance had been here last night. "You know how Fridays can be. I'm just getting ready for the after-work rush."

"Uh-huh," Julie said as she plopped her purse on the stool next to her. "And I'm sure it has nothing to do with Lance

Kendall being back in town or the fact that he was here with you until around three thirty or four o'clock in the morning. Well after closing time."

Damn it.

"It's not what you think." Brynn shot Julie a sideways glance, knowing she'd already lost this round of the debate. "Did you know that Lance found pictures of numerous young girls, including Sophia and Emma?"

"That's all anyone on the hospital staff was talking about last night. Do the authorities really believe that Arthur Fetter is a serial killer? Those photographs were planted there. They had to be. Anyone with half a brain can figure that out for themselves. The killer must have put them there when he found out that Lance was getting the place. What they need to do is search the rest of the houses their daddy bought them and see what comes up."

Brynn got what she wanted by averting the conversation from Lance, but this topic wasn't any better than the one before. It was all she'd thought about last night. Well, when she hadn't been obsessing over whether or not she'd made the right decision in turning Lance down on his dinner invitation.

"I can't imagine being able to accept the idea that Arthur would do something like that," Brynn replied honestly, taking a handful of the cocktail napkins, spiraling a stack, and then setting them by the small tray of fresh oranges, limes, lemons, and cherries for mixed drinks. "There has to be some other reason those pictures were in his house, and I can't believe someone would frame the Kendalls."

"I'm not surprised another news crew arrived in town this morning." Julie shook her head in response to the menu Brynn tried to slide her way. "No, thanks. I can't stay long. My shift at the hospital starts in an hour. So that's why Lance stopped by last night, huh? To tell you about the pictures he'd found? Nothing more?"

Brynn should have known Julie wouldn't allow the conversation to stray too far from her scoop about Lance Kendall's early morning visit. She sighed in acceptance and set the box with the rest of the cocktail napkins onto the top of the cabinet. She'd store them in the back later.

A quick glance at the few patrons eating wings told her that everyone was still enjoying their lunch. No one needed a refill quite yet, so she could spare a couple minutes being roasted over the coals.

"Lance was driving through town from his new home to his dad's house when he decided to stop in for a last-minute drink. Lord knows he needed it after the night he had. Of course, I was closing up the bar, so we shared a drink as friends. Nothing more." Brynn pulled out the stool from underneath the bar and took a seat. She was exhausted, and the day was only getting started. "We didn't even really have a chance to get caught up. I mean, can you imagine the shock he must have experienced at finding those photographs?"

"What if they're just pictures left behind and they have no connection to Sophia or Emma?" Julie reached over and lifted the clear, segmented lid to gain access to the compartment with the cherries. She popped one into her mouth and used her teeth to hold it while she pulled out the stem. "I mean, there were other photographs in the stack. Are the rest of the girls missing too? Let's face it. Everyone is on edge and it was only a matter of time before someone started to point the finger at someone. We're talking about an eighty-something year old man who everyone loved and considered part of the local gentry. That is, as far as the farming community goes. There could be a reasonable explanation as to why those pictures were in his house. We just aren't in a position to know yet."

Brynn didn't have to point out that there were a lot of towns like theirs where the residents were shocked at finding out who the suspect was who had committed some horrifying crime. Blyth Lake wasn't alone, nor would they be the last to discover that their Norman Rockwell town wasn't quite as picturesque as they'd thought.

"I'm not saying that I can possibly imagine in my wildest dreams a rational explanation for Arthur to be looking at pictures of a bunch of missing girls," Julie clarified, pointing the cherry stem Brynn's way. "Now, what else happened last night that had you looking as if you could have shredded that box of napkins into a billion particles of confetti?"

Brynn shifted on the stool, wondering how to word what took place between herself and Lance without sounding as if she regretted her decision.

"Do you remember when Lance graduated early and left town to join the service?" Brynn might as well remind Julie of the past, because recalling how difficult that time was would go a long way in fortifying her choice to decline Lance's offer to go to dinner. "I'd known all along he was leaving, just as he understood that I wanted to stay here. It was no one's fault, but you—of all people—should remember how hard it was for me to say goodbye after all the time Lance and I spent together."

"I do remember, hon." Julie leaned forward, though it wasn't as if anyone was close enough to overhear their conversation. "What you're leaving out of that trip down memory lane is how much you loved him. You would have done anything to keep him here with you. I don't care that you were seventeen years old. Love is love. No one can deny that is what the two of you shared."

"And we've both changed so much over the last twelve

years," Brynn countered, not surprised that Julie had gone down that road. "I have a life of my own now, just as he does. Lance is basically starting over here, regardless that he grew up in Blyth Lake. Julie, he might be someone totally different from the man we all knew back then. And for all I know, he could be in a relationship with some woman."

Brynn didn't bother to say that Lance never would have asked her to dinner if that was the case, but she wasn't ready to share that part of last night with her friend. At least, not yet.

"Did Lance indicate that he was involved with someone at any point since then or now? Is that why you have hives on your chest?"

Brynn instinctively looked down at the V-neck of the black t-shirt she'd put on this morning, always in the habit of wearing something that had the Cavern's logo on the fabric. She didn't notice any hives or red blotches on her chest. It was then she realized she'd been duped.

"Damn it, Julie."

"Gotcha," Julie replied with a smile, though understanding shined bright from her blue eyes. "Fine. You're not ready to share. I get that."

It was then that Brynn noticed Julie's darker shade of lipstick. She always wore a bit of makeup during her shift as a medic, but maintained a natural look with a pale pink lip gloss. The cinnamon color she wore today was brand new.

"Turning the tables here, is there anything you want to tell me?" Brynn raised an eyebrow in question. "Is there a new guy working at the hospital I should know about? A doctor, perhaps?"

One thing about both of them being blonde was that it was easy to see when a flush adorned their cheeks.

"Do tell, my friend."

"I'll spill when you spill," Julie tried to negotiate, indicating that wouldn't be happening anytime soon as she absconded with another cherry out of the garnish tray that Brynn had just filled while snatching up her purse. She hopped off the stool a little more composed than she'd been thirty seconds prior to making her getaway. "That's what I thought, *blondie*."

Brynn could only laugh at the nickname Julie had used on purpose to make her point. It appeared they both had some things they weren't willing to share quite yet.

"Hi, Jeremy," Brynn greeted her regular, having seen him come through the heavy door after Julie passed by him as she was leaving for her shift. It came as a surprise to see that he wasn't alone. "Whitney. I thought you were out of town for the week."

"I was until I heard that my picture was in that stack of photographs Lance Kendall found last night in Arthur Fetter's basement."

Brynn really needed to get her hearing checked.

"Your picture was in…"

"You heard me right the first time," Whitney said with a dramatic sigh. She took the stool to the right of where her father always sat before pointing to the draft beers. "I'll take whatever you have freshest on tap."

Whitney and Brynn had been friends all through high school, but Whitney hadn't stayed in town the whole time. She'd left the day after graduation and only came home to visit every so many years. It was obvious that whatever path she'd taken hadn't been an easy one. She had a hardened look that only came from living life in the fast lane.

Brynn almost let it slip that Lance hadn't said anything about Whitney's picture being in the mix, but she caught herself just in time.

"How did you find out?" Brynn served up Jeremy's usual, as well as Whitney's request for a draft beer. "Did Detective Kendrick already call you?"

Brynn had spoken to the detective a couple of times over the last couple of months because of her friendship with Emma, but she had also talked with him because she'd gone to camp that summer with Sophia. Honestly, the poor detective most likely questioned every resident in Blyth Lake by this point, because everyone knew everyone else. She certainly didn't envy him his job and digging through years of Blyth Lake's dirt.

"Yes," Whitney replied before taking a long drink of her beer. She wiped away the foam on her top lip as she looked around the bar. Brynn wasn't sure who she was looking for, but the place wouldn't pick up until after five o'clock. They were still a few hours away from the first rush of patrons. "Detective Kendrick wanted to meet me this morning so that I could look at the picture. He was hoping I'd remember who'd taken it."

"Whoever took it was apparently smart enough not to catch her attention." Jeremy stared at his beer as though the malt beverage had all the answers. She was somewhat shocked when he didn't drink it right away. "You were smiling and looking away from the lens, almost as if you didn't even know the picture was being taken."

"And you don't remember anything?" Brynn was surprised that Whitney wouldn't remember Arthur Fetter taking her picture, even if she hadn't been staring directly at the camera. This might very well mean that Arthur didn't have a thing to do with Sophia's murder or Emma's disappearance. He might just be innocent as Brynn had originally suspected. "What about the clothes you were wearing? Or the way you wore your hair? Does anything suggest when the picture might have been taken?"

"Yeah, it does." Whitney took another fortifying drink, telling Brynn all she needed to know. "It was when we were at camp with Emma and Sophia. Brynn, you don't think that I was a target just like the rest of them, do you?"

CHAPTER TEN

LANCE IMMEDIATELY NOTICED that Brynn wasn't behind the bar when he came through the door. At least, he was fairly sure it wasn't her…as long as she hadn't cut her hair or gotten numerous, rather adventurous tattoos in the last twenty-four hours. Whoever the woman was manning the bar, she was doing a damned fine job from the looks of things.

It was evident that the evening crowd at the Cavern were growing in numbers as each night wore on, though it was still relatively early tonight in comparison to the after-dinner rush. Folks tended to arrive at their favorite drinking establishments after the working day was done and they'd packed away their evening meal. Considering the two-screen movie theater on Main Street had closed years ago and the nearest bowling alley was in the city, Tiny's Cavern was about it when it came to adult entertainment.

Lance suddenly realized that Brynn must be doing an all-time record-breaking profit since the body was discovered and the reporters began to congregate here every evening, milling around while talking with the locals.

Loud conversations were in process, the smack of the balls on the two recently refurbished pool tables hinted at friendly wagers, and Chad Schaeffer was in his usual spot in front of the dart boards schilling the reporters who seemed to be all too willing marks. His partner was someone Lance didn't recognize, but the man wasn't here to mingle from the look in the guy's eyes.

"Hey, have you seen Brynn?" Lance stopped a new waiter who was delivering a basket of butterflied shrimp and shoestring fries to one of the tables next to the Wurlitzer jukebox glowing in all its neon majesty. He was hoping this employee would know the answer to Brynn's whereabouts. "I need to talk to her about something important."

It was still relatively easy to hear the waiter's response over the country music blaring from the multiple surround sound speakers that Brynn had installed. The same wouldn't be true once the live band started to play tonight at twenty hundred hours since it was the opening Friday night of live entertainment.

It didn't matter that most of the booking would be the local garage bands and budding artists just getting started in the music business. Brynn was stepping up her efforts to build her tavern into a hotspot that would draw people from the surrounding small towns.

Everyone around Blyth Lake had been talking about her business plan for the Cavern since well before he'd gotten home. Hell, even his brother had remarked on her improvements.

Lance's high school girlfriend had grown into a real honest to God businesswoman.

"She's in the office."

Lance nodded his appreciation, but he didn't look forward to trying to make it across the place when everyone and their father would want to talk to him about those damned pictures he'd found. Hell, he and his dad had spent most of their lunch fending off questions from the other patrons at the diner. That didn't even account for the hour Lance and Noah had spent over at Calvin's hardware store. They'd gotten the third degree from the gathering of elderly men from around town who hung out there playing dominos for a penny a point most afternoons.

Honestly, Lance was pretty sure he'd now spoken to every single living resident within the town's limits since his return. That wouldn't stop everyone here from trying to see if there were any new developments.

"Need an escort or a riot gun?"

Lance couldn't help but smile and stick out his arm for the firm handshake only Tiny Phifer could give. The giant of a man had a death grip that could make a teenage boy piss himself in fear...which was the intended effect. Well, it appeared Lance hadn't quite seen everyone since returning to town.

"It's good to see you again, Tiny." Lance wasn't surprised when Tiny drew him in close with a slap on the back. "And seeing as you just read my mind, maybe you could clear a path. I was hoping to take Brynn out to dinner, but I'd rather it be earlier instead of closing time, which is how long it would take me to break a trail through this crowd."

Lance figured it was in his best interest to be upfront with the man. After all, Tiny was the closest thing Brynn had to family. In all regards, Tiny was Brynn's father. He'd taken her in after her parents had died, getting her through high school and even putting her through college. The man had been there through the toughest of times and regarded Brynn as the daughter he and Rose had never had in their younger years.

Lance and Tiny made their way across the main floor. No one ever bothered Tiny unless he purposefully stopped at their table to make small talk. His imposing presence prevented most interlopers from bothering either one of them. Lance felt the heavy stares of every individual, but he ignored them, as he had most of the day. There wasn't anything else he could tell them that they didn't already know. He wasn't involved in the investigation, regardless that he'd found a stack of pictures that included a number of new potential victims.

"Lance, I don't have to worry, do I?" Tiny's meaning was all too clear. "You wouldn't be stupid enough to hurt her again, would you?"

Lance hadn't thought for a fraction of a second that he would make it to Brynn's office without having a serious discussion with Tiny about his intentions. He respected Tiny for what he'd done to help Brynn and didn't doubt the man would lay him out with one haymaker to the jaw if for one second Brynn's emotions were on the line and Lance didn't show her the appropriate level of respect.

"I'll be honest with you." Lance wouldn't hold back from expressing his lack of confidence as to what the future held for them, considering her previous refusal to have dinner with him. "I truly didn't realize how very much I'd missed Brynn until I saw her again recently. I'm having a hard time getting her to say yes to dinner, let alone anything more involved. You've known me since I was a boy, Tiny. I would never intentionally hurt Brynn, and she will always have my respect."

"I understand that, but you hurt her all the same."

The glaring truth hit Lance's chest like a massive blow that could easily have knocked him into the wall if he hadn't steadied himself. He hadn't gotten off scot-free back then either, but she'd always expressed to him her support in the letters she wrote. He spent months half-believing that their break-up hadn't affected her the way it had him, but then he'd remember their last kiss, and he'd known that wasn't true.

"It was a tough time for both of us," Lance acknowledged, unable to change the past. He honestly wasn't sure he would if he was given the chance. His time in the Marines had shaped him into the man he was today, which was a far cry from the high school boy who'd left a young girl who held his heart back then and the town that would forever hold his childhood memories. "I can only say that I want to reconnect with my oldest best friend, get reacquainted with my family, and start fresh in my hometown. I spent time with Brynn last night, and it was the first time something clicked inside of me that I was finally home."

Tiny nodded his understanding. At least, Lance thought his gesture was in understanding. He might be reading the situation completely wrong.

"She's my little girl, Lance. It's my job to look out for her. If you step out of line, I'll have to put you down."

"Understood."

Lance held back from knocking on Brynn's office door. He glanced back to the bar area, noticing the band was starting to set up for their live performance. Tiny was already deep in conversation with their road manager, but Lance didn't doubt Brynn had already covered tonight's song choices.

He'd always known that she would still be in Blyth Lake when he returned, though he honestly thought she'd be married and living on the edge of town in a two-story house with a white picket fence, raising a little girl who was her exact duplicate. There was never a time that he spoke to his parents over the years that he didn't inquire about her and what life had been like for her.

Brynn had made it perfectly clear last night that she didn't think they could reclaim what they'd had in high school. She'd been right even back then when she said waiting would not be a good option for them given the distance and the time they would spend apart.

It hadn't been his intention to try and rekindle their relationship upon returning home. He sure as hell had enough priorities to occupy his time, but he'd held her in his arms last night. It was the first time he'd truly felt he was home since he'd gotten back from the war.

Granted, it was a reception that mirrored many of the other residents' outward greetings.

Yet it wasn't the same. His heart knew the difference.

"You know," Brynn said the moment she swung open her office door, "I can see your shadow underneath the door. How long were you planning on standing out there?"

"Until I figured out how to get you to say yes to my dinner invitation."

"Good luck with that."

And just like that, Brynn closed the door in his face.

Lance was lucky he'd pulled back in the nick of time, or else he would have ended up with a broken nose and an unexpected trip to the hospital. He couldn't help but smile at the fire she just sparked underneath him with the dare she'd laid out before him.

"I don't need luck," Lance announced, opening the door and crossing the threshold with a renewed sense of determination. "It's actually pretty simple, really."

"Oh yeah?" Brynn settled back into her office chair behind her desk, but the tilt of her head and the sparkle in those brown eyes of hers let him know that she was curious about his tactics. "And how is getting me to have dinner with you simple when I've already turned you down, Einstein?"

Lance took a moment to study her, though it was more to give himself time to back off this path he was currently considering launching himself down. It hadn't been his intention to hurt her when they were younger, just as he would never deliberately do so now.

But what was so wrong with wanting to reconnect with her, whether it be a simple friendship or to maybe grow it into something more?

Brynn's pretty pink lips parted as if she were going to say something, only to then close them after reconsideration. The desire to taste her was too strong to resist, and he slowly closed the distance between them.

"What do you think you're doing?" Brynn stood up so abruptly that her chair rolled back into the wall. She held up a finger in warning. "You can stop right there, Lance Kendall. What are you up to?"

"It's simple." Lance did stop when he was mere inches from her. He'd always respected her wishes, and he would continue to do so. "Kiss me."

"I'm sorry?"

"Kiss me. If you feel nothing, I'll head to the bar to drown my sorrows, knowing we'll only ever be friends from this moment on." Lance noticed that Brynn stopped breathing, though he was relatively certain that was the start of the reaction he was looking for tonight. "If you feel even the slightest flicker of the flames that are currently burning inside of me, then I get to take you to dinner."

"I could lie."

"You wouldn't. You can't."

"This is foolish." Brynn finally took a deep breath, though he could hear the slight catch in her throat. She wasn't immune to what was still between them, either. "We're both adults who can make decisions without relying on our hormones to drive our actions."

Lance remained where he was, maintaining his level stare, proving that he would wait for her acquiesce before kissing her.

"This is so ridiculous," Brynn said rather impatiently after another minute had passed. Had she really thought he'd give up and walk away? "Fine. It won't change anything."

Lance smiled in victory, yet he would never let her know that he was trembling with anticipation. He'd thought of this moment for many, many years...and that epiphany alone suggested he'd subconsciously waited for her all these years.

He gradually stepped forward, never releasing her gaze.

"One kiss," Lance murmured, slowly raising his hand so that he could cradle her beautiful face in his palm. He could literally feel her heart beating in time with his as he pulled her close to him. "I really have truly missed you, blondie."

Lance didn't give her time to respond. He closed his lips over hers, swearing that the sky had opened up overheard with an incredibly impressive fireworks show to rival the Fourth of July on the centennial. He wrapped one arm around her lower waist, needing something to balance them as they formed their bodies together for the first time since their youth.

How was it that she could still taste like fresh strawberries after all this time?

Lance didn't bother to suppress a moan of satisfaction when the tip of her tongue barely traced over his lower lip. He couldn't get enough of her. It was as if he were a newborn vampire with a thirst he just couldn't quench.

"Hey, Brynn, the credit card machine isn't—oh, shit! Sorry."

Lance immediately dropped his hands and stepped back, not wanting Brynn to be caught in an awkward situation by one of her new employees. Talk about being doused with ice water at the exact wrong moment.

"It's fine, Kristen." Brynn leaned forward against the desk, giving him the slightest bit of satisfaction. Hell, he was using the wall for support. The woman who interrupted them was the same one who'd been bartending when he'd walked in earlier. "I'll check to see if the Wi-Fi went down."

"Thanks for that," Kristen said rather sheepishly before she quickly took two steps back and closed the door.

Heavy silence hung in the air. Lance couldn't prevent the previous tension from settling in his shoulders. Had she not been affected by their kiss? He sure as hell was still reeling from the distant past and current emotions slamming into one another.

"So, where are you taking me to dinner?"

CHAPTER ELEVEN

"**Y**OU CAN'T BE serious."

"I am." Brynn settled back against the arm of her couch, careful not to spill the red liquid over the rim of her wine glass. She needed every drop she could get. "We signed the papers months ago, but the process of me taking over the Cavern started a couple of years back. Tiny and Rose want to travel more, but they also took on quite the project up at the lake. It only made sense for me to buy them out so they could diversify into a business that was better able to accommodate their plans."

Brynn pulled her legs underneath her so that both of them had room on the cushions. She and Lance had come up to her apartment, not wanting to have dinner at the diner. And she certainly wasn't leaving town on a Friday night when the bar was so busy. She honestly wasn't ready to fend off the questions that would no doubt circulate had she and Lance gone to eat at Annie's Diner. The smart thing was to come upstairs with some burgers, yet still be accessible to Kristen and the staff if need be.

She had reminded herself several times over the last hour that this was only a friendly dinner. She needed to keep repeating that sentiment over and over, because each brush of his hand and each shared look made her apartment seem as if it didn't have any air in it at all, let alone central air.

"Your major was in business, but I never in a million years

would have guessed that you would own the Cavern. I would have thought your long-term plan included Tiny and Rose as silent partners." Lance rested his right arm over the back of the couch so that they were facing one another. He'd run his hand through his hair at one point, so it was slightly ruffled on top even though the sides were cut short. It gave him a just-rolled-out-of-bed look that caused Brynn to yearn for more than conversation about what she'd been doing for the past twelve years. "I guess it makes sense, though. You're surrounded by family every night of the week."

No one else had made the connection. At least, she didn't think the townsfolk had come to that conclusion.

Brynn realized that she'd created a point system in her head on whether or not this dinner should extend into another. He'd just garnered another notch, because his theory on why she wanted the bar was spot on. It proved that he still had insight to her that others didn't and never would have.

"Everyone in our tiny village, so to speak, seemed to have a hand in making sure I stayed on the straight and narrow after Mom and Dad died." It was a lot easier to talk about her parents now than it had been when she'd been younger. It was even more effortless to reminisce how everyone had gathered around her, never once letting her slip through the cracks. Isn't that what family did for one another? "Every face that walks through that door had a hand in me going to college one way or another. I owe this town and its people so much."

Brynn wasn't talking figuratively either. She'd discovered upon graduating high school that the town had taken up a collection to put her through college after her parents died, and any tips left for Tiny over the years at the Cavern went into that same fund. She'd been able to graduate debt free, and now she'd come home to return the favor—by giving back to the same town that had supported her in her time of need. She'd even started a scholarship fund for some lucky student who needed it somewhere down the road in years to come.

"Have you spoken to Shae?"

Brynn's heart squeezed upon hearing the name of her best friend's sister. Emma would always be her best friend, regardless that she had disappeared. Brynn and Julie still got together every year on the day Emma went missing to reminisce about their friend, making sure her memory was never forgotten. They even made a point of talking to anyone they met on those occasions about Emma and her childhood in Blyth Lake.

"I haven't spoken to Shae in ages. I honestly think it hurts her to hear my voice." Brynn sipped her wine as she struggled to find the right words to explain why their calls had ceased years ago. "Let's face it. Those calls were more for me anyway."

"I think Gwen does business with Shae once in a while." Lance leaned forward and picked up his bottle of beer, though it had to be relatively warm by now. "So, you're still close with Julie?"

"I am." Brynn couldn't help but smile thinking Julie had most likely already been informed about this little dinner taking place above the bar, not to mention the kiss that had been interrupted. "She's a medic and currently partners with Billy Stanton."

"I'd heard about that from Noah," Lance replied with a shake of his head. She didn't have to ask why he was dumbfounded by her declaration. "I'm surprised Stanton stayed in town."

"We all were, but I'm not complaining."

"Let me guess," Lance said with one of those smiles that took her back in time. "He's known for buying rounds when he's lit."

"And it's usually on a Friday night when he's not on shift." Brynn left out that Billy's father consistently picked up his tab. It went unspoken, though everyone in town was well aware of the Stantons' personal business. "Word has it that Billy made an offer to Noah for his newly acquired property."

"Yeah, I'd heard the same thing." Lance didn't appear too pleased with the deal Billy tried to strike with Noah. His perplexity turned out to be about something bigger. "I'd almost forgotten how the mechanics of a small town like this works. It's one big oiled machine for people of means, isn't it?"

Brynn didn't need to answer, because Lance wasn't looking for a response.

"Is it a hard adjustment from what you were living?"

Brynn could have kicked herself, because they'd been staying on surface topics that didn't delve too deep. She'd inquired about something very personal after she'd warned herself over and over to keep things casual between them.

"It is," Lance replied softly, twisting the bottle of beer in his hands more for something to do than reading the label as it appeared he was doing. "It sounds crazy, but I was so looking forward to coming back home for a fresh start. Now that I'm here, I feel a little askew. I miss my unit, the hardships, and the camaraderie we all had."

"You have that with your family, though," Brynn pointed out, unable to stop herself from speaking her mind. She could see the longing on his features, and it was heartbreaking. "Your dad, your brothers, and your sister are like a unit by themselves."

Some of the crowd they used to hang with back in the day had long ago left Blyth Lake. There were a few still around, such as Chad Schaeffer and Billy Stanton. No one had excluded Billy back then in spite of himself, but it went unwritten where they stood when it came to the depth of their friendship. As long as someone could benefit Billy from his viewpoint, then all was good at the time.

"They are definitely a force to be reckoned with, aren't they?" Lance smiled fondly, though it was clear the type of amity he was referring to in regard to his team was different than that of his family. "I'll adjust, but I know it will take time."

How many times had she seen documentaries or the news cover the topic of PTSD in military men and women? Too many times to count, that's for sure. The instinct to ask if he suffered from the same disorder was there, but she also respected his right to privacy considering their recent revival of their friendship. They were just beginning to know one another again, and though there wasn't a rulebook for this type of thing, she didn't want to jeopardize what there was between the two of them for what could only be a small measure of insight. The right time would come for such questions. She only hoped it wouldn't be in crisis.

The band Brynn hired had started playing over an hour ago, the deep bass coming through the floorboards of her apartment. It was rather soothing to know that the bar was running effectively with her behind the black curtain. It enabled her to do a myriad of other things, such as having dinner with a man who still had the ability to break her heart.

"I should get back downstairs," Brynn said with a tinge of regret. She really had enjoyed this time with him, but it would be so easy to forget where she'd set her initial boundaries. It was time to put a little distance between them so that their momentum didn't overcome them. "Are you staying for a bit or are you heading to your dad's house?"

"I was thinking of staying."

Brynn's heart skipped a beat at his last word. It suggested a hell of a lot more than having a drink downstairs in the bar with some of his old buddies, but she managed to inspect the contents of her wine glass and pretend otherwise. She even brought up the investigation so that it kept both of them distracted from the underlying physical attraction they'd avoided throughout their meal.

"Whitney stopped in around lunchtime." Brynn drained the rest of her wine before unfolding her legs off the couch. She set her empty Styrofoam dinner container on top of his and then took them into her small kitchen. The open layout made it convenient to carry on the conversation. "You didn't mention that her picture was included with the others you found. I was thinking maybe the photos have nothing to do with Sophia Morton's murder."

"Detective Kendrick called me earlier and said he spoke with Arthur Fetter on the phone. He claims he has no knowledge of any pictures being hidden inside the furnace." Lance followed her and leaned against the counter as she rinsed out her wine glass. A quick glance told her that his piercing blue eyes were taking in every small movement she made, but his knowing smile told her she wasn't fooling him with her change in topic. "Kendrick isn't so sure the photographs are related either, but he's still pursuing them as a potential lead."

"Eleven years is a long time for a murder to go unsolved." Brynn held out her hand for his empty beer bottle. He slowly relinquished his hold on the brown glass. "Add another year for how long Emma has been missing. The connection between Sophia and Emma is definitely there, but that same list of suspects contains most of the people we know and grew up with. It's hard to wrap my mind around that fact."

"Spend tomorrow morning with me."

It was a good thing that she was tossing the beer bottle in the recycling can underneath her sink, because the glass slipped from her fingers at that precise moment.

"I wish I could." Brynn masked the trembling of her hand by closing the cabinet door and flashing him a regretful smile. "I have to conduct a couple interviews around eleven o'clock. I need to add to the Cavern's weekend staff roster."

"So that means you're free for breakfast and a tour of the new house," Lance reasoned with a grin that expressed his victory in turning the tables. "I'll pick you up around eight and then we'll head to the diner together."

Brynn bit her lip as he turned and started to walk through her living room to the door that would lead them downstairs. The band had played a number of popular, catchy songs already, but they switched to a softer ballad as if on cue. Their timing sucked as far as she was concerned, but she still managed to catch up with Lance and stop him before he exited her apartment.

"Why?" Brynn blurted out, pulling back her hand from the warmth of his arm. She wanted to berate him for looking so damned good, but she was more concerned with the direction he was taking them. "Lance, you just got back to town. There are a lot of things you could be concentrating on, such as spending time with your family and renovating your new home. It's not like I'm going anywhere, and we can't just pick up where we left off. It doesn't work that way."

There. Brynn finally said what she'd been wanting to put out there all evening. She crossed her arms and stood her ground. She'd been off balance ever since he'd returned to town. It would be nice to be back on steady ground and stick to the plan she'd laid out for her future.

"Tiny asked me what my intentions were toward you."

There was no stopping the embarrassment that flushed her face. On one hand, Tiny's concern was touching and it warmed her to know he still looked out for her wellbeing. On the other hand, she was mortified. Tiny presumptively assumed Lance wanted something more than friendship.

Did he?

Brynn stifled a groan in confusion, because she wasn't even sure what *this* was between them yet herself.

"Do you want to know what I told him?"

Not really.

A tremor of arousal traveled down her spine at the rich tone of his voice. It didn't help that he stepped forward and slowly brushed the back of his knuckles against her cheek. Yes, she desperately wanted to know what his answer had been, but something held her back from telling him the truth. It didn't matter, because he bared his soul to her anyway.

"I told him that spending time with you was the first time I truly felt like I was home." Lance surprised her when he leaned forward and softly pressed his lips against her forehead. It was something he used to do after walking her to class. She was being drawn back to their past, and there wasn't a thing she could do about resisting his efforts. "And it feels damned good, Brynn."

Frighteningly good, but she didn't say that aloud. At least, she didn't think she did.

"I'll be running on five hours of sleep," Brynn warned, her thoughts swirling with how she would handle all the questions thrown her way. There was no doubt that everyone in the bar was kibitzing about what they were doing up here, besides eating dinner. Had they taken much more time, she was sure the more creative stories would begin to circulate. It probably would have been better to go to the diner. "You sure you want to be around me that early in the morning?"

"There's no other place I'd rather be in this whole wide world, blondie."

CHAPTER TWELVE

"**Y**OU LASTED LONGER than I thought you would."
Noah ever so gently pulled back on his cue stick before smoothly stroking forward and connecting the chalked tip with the cue ball. He pocketed the number three in the corner pocket and lined up his next shot perfectly with just enough angle to give him the leave he needed for the next. Lance had forgotten how good his brother was at playing pool and already regretted betting five bucks on this game. Well, at least he wouldn't have to buy the next round as well.

"What the hell does that mean?" Lance took a swig of his beer as he sought out Brynn who was currently behind the bar with a smile on her face. He'd missed that bit of sunshine in his life and hadn't realized how much until now. "We dated in high school and remained friends. Is it a crime to get reacquainted?"

"No, but it sure as hell will be justifiable homicide when Tiny lays you out with an upper cut. He warned you, didn't he?" Noah successfully ended the first game of what was about to turn into *best out of three*. "Have you seen the size of his fists? I wouldn't put money on which blow will be the telling one…maybe the first, possibly the second."

Lance didn't bother to answer his brother's taunt, because it would only fuel Noah's need to continue on this topic of discussion. And right now, talking about Brynn was off limits. Everyone and their father was here tonight. It mostly had to do with the fact that news about him finding photographs of young girls had made the rounds and everyone wanted to be there for the next episode of the Kendall family saga. He didn't need to add fuel to the fire.

The band was still playing country music, conversation and laughter had become louder as the night wore on, and it was apparent that Brynn was making a killing tonight from the amount of alcohol that was flowing through the bar. It didn't surprise him to see the door swing open to admit more patrons.

"Did you see who just walked in the front entrance?"

"Yeah," Noah replied before thinning his lips. "Rose should have minded her own business. This family reunion isn't going to go quite as she'd planned."

Wes and Clayton Schaeffer made their way to the bar after stopping to greet several people. A quick glance in that direction told Lance that Miles had already been alerted to the fact that his two older boys had entered the premises. He was already reaching for his wallet.

"Can I buy you a drink?"

Lance thought the tall redhead was talking to someone else before realizing her question was directed toward him. She didn't look familiar and those form-fitting jeans she was sporting told him she'd purchased them recently. The fabric was way too stiff.

"I appreciate the offer, but I have a beer coming this way."

Lance had been keeping an eye on Brynn, as well as the Schaeffers. Chad had already made his way to his dad's side to fend off any confrontations. It was Reese that he finally spotted to get him out of this awkward situation. She was carrying three bottles of beer as she made her way back to the pool table.

"We have no statement to make nor comment to give, Ms. Winston," Noah said in a steel tone that told Lance this woman wasn't a tourist or a relative of someone in town.

"I wasn't looking for either," the redhead stated with sideways glance toward Noah. His assumption annoyed her, but she recovered quickly. "Believe it or not, I'm not working tonight. I was just trying to be friendly like the rest of the folks here in this small town."

"Friendly went by the wayside when you slanted your last story to suggest that Sophia basically asked to be killed because she wasn't happy at home. So, we'd appreciate it if you gave us a wide berth tonight." Reese had arrived, and she certainly wasn't a fan of the woman. Lance had already deduced that she was with one of the media crews slinking around town from Noah denying her the common courtesy of a greeting. "You don't know a thing about my family, Charlene, so please keep your distance."

"I know what it's like not to be happy with one's home life." Charlene shifted her weight on a pair of black pumps that looked to be as new as the jeans she was wearing. Something in her expression told him that she related to Sophia on a deeper level than she'd like, but whatever she'd written or said in the news mustn't have come across in that manner. "It wasn't my intention to suggest it was Sophia's fault she was murdered. It's obvious she was in the wrong place at the wrong time. I'm just doing my job."

Lance had no doubt that Reese would have told the woman that she could go and do her job somewhere else, but there was no need. Charlene Winston walked away with her head held high to an occupied table up against the front window. He didn't recognize them, so he assumed the man she'd joined was either her cameraman or hired security.

"I take it neither one of you are fans of Ms. Winston." Lance reached for the rack and began collecting the pool balls. "Anyone else I need to watch out for around here? I mean, besides the serial killer we seem to have discovered."

"Charlene is the only one who's hung around town on a consistent basis," Reese responded, having already handed Noah a beer and put the other one on the table they'd claimed next to where they were playing pool. "I'm going back to the bar to talk to Kristen. Did you know she wants to go back to school to be a teacher?"

Noah caught Reese's elbow before she could walk away, bringing her in close for a kiss and causing her to laugh. His smile said it all, and Lance was somewhat envious at the ease in which his brother had acclimated to civilian life.

"It's odd, isn't it?" Lance asked, carefully lifting the rack and stowing it back in place before reaching for his beer. He surveyed the patrons carefully, noting the regular customers from those who were virtually strangers. "How everything has changed, and yet things still seem the same as when we left?"

"It takes a while, Lance." Noah had been paying attention. Both of them were more aware of their surroundings than they had been back when life had been simple. "Give it time."

Lance was surprised to find Clayton and Miles deep in conversation while Wes stayed at the bar and Chad resumed his game of darts. Had Rose been right in hiring Wes and Clayton to build more cottages up at the lake, while Miles and Chad restored the existing ones? Would this bring the broken family back together or only cause the rift to widen?

"Who's playing darts with Chad?" Lance asked, trying to familiarize himself with the changes to the Cavern's clientele here in Blyth Lake. It also kept the conversation off his relationship with Brynn. "That's not someone we went to school with, is it?"

Noah didn't even have to look across the bar to know who Lance was referring to in his inquiry.

"Irish. He bought the garage on the corner of Main and Sixth Street around a year ago." Noah took the break, sending one of the solids into the side pocket. "I hear he's pretty good with a wrench."

"Old man Delaney finally retire?"

"No," Noah said with a bit of regret. "He up and died from a heart attack."

"Shit," Lance muttered with a shake of his head. So many changes. "The evening just took a turn for the worse."

Lance hadn't meant to mess up Noah's shot, but one glimpse of Sheriff Percy as he came strolling through the door had the seven-ball missing the side pocket by at least two inches.

"He's a stupid, lazy son of a bitch." Noah stepped away from the table and leaned an elbow on the back of a stool as he settled in to observe the sheriff. Percy joined Chester and Harlan in the booth they were occupying with their wives. "Byron Warner has taken over Percy's duties as sheriff while the board decides what to do with him. He royally fucked up when he didn't check on why Deputy Wallace didn't do his check-in for hours after the beginning of his shift. Hell, it probably cost the man his life. People out here don't understand rank equals responsibility and not power to do as you please."

"Dad told me he's been trying to talk Mitch into running for the position once he gets home." Lance noticed that Brynn was switching her attention between Miles' conversation with Clayton and the table Sheriff Percy decided to join. "I think it's a great idea, but you realize there could be a major obstacle with Mitch following that suggestion."

"The fact that I found a body in the drywall of my new home, and you found the victim's picture in yours?" Noah took a long draw of his beer before setting the bottle down with a thud. "Yeah, it's occurred to me that might be a problem for our big brother. Maybe conflict of interest or something like that. The Kendall name definitely got caught up in this investigation real quick."

Brynn came out from behind the bar and slowly made her way across the floor. She stopped by a few tables to check on her customers, but it was clear she had a destination in mind. It appeared her final destination was Charlene Winston's table. Lance was taken aback when Brynn leaned in close to make a very clear point about something important.

What the hell was going on?

"You going to take your turn or are you forfeiting?"

Lance shot an irritated look Noah's way before starting what was a decent run on his stripes. He cleaned the table and sunk the eight ball before Brynn finished talking to the news anchor. It wasn't that much of a surprise to see Charlene and her cameraman leave shortly afterward.

"Rack 'em." Lance laid his cue across the pool table before making his way toward Brynn. She was halfway back to the bar before he caught her. "What was that all about, blondie? Everything okay or is something afoot?"

"All is good now." Brynn flashed a not-so-innocent smile and patted him on the chest. "I'm just looking out for my own people. Go back to playing pool with your brother, Sherlock. I've got to say, Lance, it's nice having you back around."

She surprised him once again when she patted his backside and continued to the bar, where Tiny was engaged in conversation with Jeremy Bell. Lance breathed a sigh of relief that the man's back was toward him, but his respite was short-lived when their gazes clashed in the mirror above the bar.

Tiny had his eye on him. Lance wasn't getting away with one damned thing.

"Damn it, blondie," Lance muttered in frustration underneath his breath before turning back toward his brother. He didn't have to look at Tiny's hand to see how large his fist was or the fact that just one impact would hurt like hell. "Noah, did I ever tell you that you're an asshole and a terrible brother?"

CHAPTER THIRTEEN

"I T WASN'T REALLY that much of a big deal," Brynn laughed at Lance's stunned reaction. She rested her forearm in the open window of Lance's truck, enjoying the morning's warmth from the sun. He was driving them to his new house, but not if he kept taking his eyes off the road to look at her as if she'd just grown horns out of her head. "It was two dates. Three, at the most."

"You dated Byron Warner."

"Yes." Brynn bubbled with laughter again as Lance made it sound like she'd committed the worst crime possible by spending some time out with a sweet guy. It was the same reaction he had when Byron stopped by their table at the diner to say hello, all but suggesting that he and Brynn should get together for another meal sometime soon. "He really is a nice guy. He was a complete gentleman, and he doesn't condone how Sheriff Percy runs the department at all. We just weren't compatible. We're better as friends."

It was kind of fun to see him struggle with the vision of a goodnight kiss. Her smile widened when his grip tightened on the steering wheel.

"You're at a disadvantage, because you personally know every man I've dated. Well, except for when I was in college," Brynn pointed out, really enjoying this conversation. The honeysuckles that Ms. Barmore had planted throughout the town were no longer in season, but the air remained sweet with various flowers still in bloom this late in the season. "I wouldn't know any of the women you've dated, nor would I want to, but it really doesn't matter."

"Doesn't it? How's that?"

The way Lance worded his question stole her breath, because he was once again signifying that there was something more between them than friendship. Maybe there was the beginnings of something. After all, she'd spent most of last night watching him play pool and enjoying the view immensely.

"What I think is that we both agreed to take our growing friendship day by day," Brynn reminded him, leaning forward and turning up the radio as they drove toward the old Fetter place. She'd have to get that label out of her head, considering the house was Lance's new home. The song ended right as they came up to his driveway. "Is there much work to be done?"

"Not so much as you'd think, but it will still take me around a month to repaint, update, and rewire most of the house." Lance parked the truck in front of the unattached one-car garage, staring at the house with a bit of disbelief. "It's surreal that my parents did this for all us kids."

"Do Jace, Mitch, and Gwen know your father and mother purchased them property as well?" Brynn had always pictured the Kendalls as a lot like the Waltons. She loved watching the reruns on television. She used to try and imitate some of the story lines with her parents, but they were constantly traveling on their missionary trips. She gave up trying for the perfect family around the age of nine. "I bet they're excited to be coming home to Blyth Lake."

"They don't even know that Noah and I received our homes as gifts." Lance removed the truck keys and opened the driver side door. It wasn't until he'd made his way around the bed of the truck and opened her door that she could see he wasn't comfortable with keeping the truth from his siblings. "Gwen left a message last night asking how I got the down payment for closing when I didn't touch any of the mutual funds in my portfolio. I haven't called her back, because I don't want to lie to her."

"You're not still scared of your sister, are you, Lance?" Brynn teased, hopping down from the cab of the truck and losing her breath when Lance didn't step back right away. The warmth from his body was a lot hotter than the morning sun. She wanted to soak in his heat, but she reminded herself that she wasn't seventeen anymore. And he wasn't the same young teenager, either. "You should call Gwen back so that she doesn't get suspicious. Just tell her you didn't need a down payment. Maybe she'll assume you used your VA loan. If she asks you straight out, tell her it was something like that. She doesn't need to know all the details."

"Change of subject here, but thank you for spending time with me this morning." Lance reached up and took a hold of one of her curls, wrapping the end of the strand around his finger. There was a sadness in his eyes that caused her heart to ache for this difficult transition back into the civilian world. He wiped his sorrow away with the smallest lift to the corner of his lips. "Byron doesn't know what he's missing."

Brynn didn't argue with Lance, because to do so would reveal that she was the one who distanced herself after only a couple of dates. Byron Warner was older by five or six years, but he was a little too set in his ways for Brynn. She wasn't the type to kiss and tell, or in this case dine, so she remained silent as Lance led the way to the white pillared porch.

Lance held his arms up in the air with a sparkle of excitement in those blue eyes of his, reminding her of a kid in a candy store.

"Well, what do you think? It has potential, right?"

"I think a simple gallon or two of paint can make this place look brand new," Brynn said, admiring the fact that the house was in better shape than she would have guessed after sitting empty for so long. "Calvin is going to love having you Kendalls back and fixing up every old house in town."

Calvin Arlos owned the only hardware store in town. Granted, he liked to keep his own hours due to his love of fishing, but he could get his hands on practically anything anyone needed for a renovation such as this. The Kendalls weren't known for outsourcing their labor, so it was already assumed they would do their own restorations. At least, most of the ones that didn't require a qualified tradesman. Even most of that work would be done and only need to be inspected and signed off on the building permit by a licensed journeyman. She knew about all that tedious knowledge from the repairs Tiny and Rose had done themselves up at the lake.

"I think Noah's business over the last couple of months alone is going to buy Calvin that new fishing boat he's been talking about," Lance said wryly, choosing a key on his keyring before even opening the screen door. "Add in the order I'm about to place and he might actually be able to buy his own dock instead of the one he rents from Tiny and Rose."

Brynn had never before been inside Arthur Fetter's residence, but she hadn't expected the living room to be so large in the old farmhouse. The staircase that led up to the second floor was absolutely stunning—solid hardwood worn with time. It only needed a coat of good stain to be brought back to life once again. She could already picture in her mind the matching wood furniture Lance would no doubt make with his own hands.

"Lance," Brynn murmured as she walked around the room

and toward the staircase. "This is truly beautiful."

Lance gave her a tour and painted a vision of warm colors, welcoming handmade furniture, and a décor that would envelop guests with open arms. A few of his ideas would require more than a few weeks and some paint, but at least he'd be able to move in while finishing up most of the renovations. She honestly couldn't wait to see the finished product.

His phone rang right when she'd opened the door to the basement.

"Gwen?" Brynn guessed from the aggravated look on Lance's face. He never was one to lie, which was usually why he ended up grounded back in high school. "Just answer her call and get it over with."

"Easier for you to say," Lance grumbled, swiping the display on his phone before pressing it to his ear. "Hey, sis. How are things going?"

Brynn motioned that she was going to finish her tour before flipping the switch to the lightbulb above the stairwell. She could only imagine how dark it would be had it been nighttime, but it was clear there was a window due to the sunshine lighting the bottom of the steps. She could see why Lance would want to rewire some of the electricity, especially if he were to finish the basement properly. As it stood, Arthur Fetter must have only used the basement for storage and shelter during storms.

It was decent-sized, and she could easily picture this being made into some type of game room, maybe with a pool table or a large television where he and his siblings could watch a football game while ragging one another. She stood in the middle of the room picturing another scene from the Waltons when something shiny caught her attention in the corner by the window.

Was that broken glass?

Brynn walked closer to where one of the daylight windows

was installed, instantly noticing the change in temperature and the rise in humidity. Half the window had been shattered and part of the frame was damaged. The lever was clearly not latched, and it didn't take a genius to figure out someone had broken into the house very recently.

"Lance!" Brynn spun around in dread and scoured the entire basement, figuring there could only be one hiding place. She'd seen enough horror movies to know she shouldn't walk to the back of the cellar and underneath the stairs. Whoever had broken in could easily be hiding behind the furnace. "Lance, come down here quick!"

Brynn never took her eyes off the furnace unit underneath the stairs, not even when she heard Lance quickly descending the steps. Too many things had happened around Blyth Lake recently to take this type of thing lightly, especially considering what Lance had found inside this very house.

"Brynn, are you okay?" Lance asked worriedly, still holding his phone as he searched the basement for any reason she would have called out to him in fright. His gaze immediately landed on the broken glass and he held up his hand in warning as he walked directly to the only place one could hide down here. She braced herself for someone to rush forward and all but tackle Lance to the concrete floor, but nothing like that happened as he finished his short-lived search. "Son of a bitch."

"What?" Brynn quickly stepped forward to see what had caught Lance's attention. "What is it?"

"The cover to the furnace filter has been removed." Lance reached out to show her, but was very careful not to touch the metal plate. His fingerprints were already on the metal, but he wouldn't want to contaminate any other prints that the police may be able to obtain. "See? Someone didn't slide the cover back onto these two tracks properly."

Brynn looked over her shoulder at the damage to the window, wondering why someone would want to explore the same area where Lance had discovered the photographs. Her stomach revolted in disgust. The police had already combed through the grounds quite thoroughly. She suppressed the slightest of shivers.

Had the police missed something in their search that the killer wanted to retrieve? Did those pictures actually belong to the killer in the first place? Had he come back to place more evidence that could implicate Lance's guilt?

She couldn't stop her imagination from working overtime.

"Detective Kendrick?" Lance's greeting on the phone had Brynn looking back at him to gauge his reaction to the detective's response. "We have a problem. Someone broke into my house last night and messed with the furnace where I found the small tin of pictures. You might want to have your forensics team come back here to dust for prints, or search for whatever evidence that may have been left behind. No, I haven't touched it."

Brynn would have said yesterday that the pictures could have easily been mementos, though she couldn't come up with a valid excuse as to why someone would have hidden them inside a furnace or its ductwork, let alone Arthur. It made no sense. So why in the world would some stranger have...

"That's it," Brynn exclaimed excitedly, resting a hand on Lance's shoulder. He was listening intently to what Detective Kendrick had to say on the other end of the line, but this couldn't wait. "Lance, ask him if it's possible if someone planted those pictures to throw suspicion on Arthur or to shift blame onto the Kendall family."

"Brynn Mercer is here with me." Lance didn't have to explain who she was, considering she'd spoken to Detective

Kendrick over a month ago about Emma's disappearance. Brynn hadn't been able to add anything that hadn't been in the original report, but she still held out hope that a fresh set of eyes might see something now that hadn't been seen before. "Yes, sir. I'll be here."

"Well?" Brynn assumed that Detective Kendrick was on his way out here, but she'd love to know what he thought of her suggestion. "Does he think it's possible?"

"First, let me just say I don't like the excitement in your voice at thinking a serial killer is coming in and out of my house as if he owns the place." Lance's gaze drifted over the shards of glass in anger. "Second, Kendrick said he's taking everything into consideration. He isn't excluding any possibilities. He's on his way, along with another forensic tech."

"Lance, you're misunderstanding me," Brynn argued with a shake of her head. She waved a hand toward the window. "This proves that Arthur Fetter isn't the serial killer. One, he's in Florida right now. Two, he's not in good enough health to break a window, crawl through it and drop four feet onto the concrete floor without breaking a hip, and then have the strength to hoist himself back up there on the ledge if he used the same way to get out."

"That's what worries me, Brynn." Lance shot a quick glance of concern her way. "If Arthur Fetter isn't the one we've been looking for, then the serial killer is most likely still here in Blyth Lake."

CHAPTER FOURTEEN

"I HEARD THROUGH the grapevine that you had quite a day."

"You could say that," Lance muttered, having already gone through today's events four times. Five, if he wanted to count his run-in with Byron Warner. That was a conversation Lance would rather forget, though he figured he had gotten his point across concerning Brynn. "How are you doing, Calvin?"

Noah had already gone into the city and bought two brand new security windows for the basement daylight slots. Only one of the old casements had its frame damaged, but the previous two were matching styles and neither had the capability of keeping out a teenage boy with a screwdriver, let alone a man with motive.

The new full-sized frames had a fine micro-lattice of Graphene wire between the double panes of glass, making it nearly impossible to enter the house through them even after the glass was broken out.

Noah ended up saving Lance the time needed to make such a trip while he handled the foot traffic through his house once again. He'd already researched the best local high-tech security companies around the area, pleased when he was also able to schedule an appointment to have the security system installed at the beginning of next week.

Lance had actually identified the basement windows as a likely avenue of approach for intruders when he filled out the security questionnaire. He indicated he wanted trembler units on each of the windows with a motion sensor mounted on a wall opposite them for those times when he was away from home. It provided a layered approach to the system and made defeating the network of devices much more difficult.

The system came with a predetermined amount of detecting units and features. However, he'd added numerous additional line items and a full complement of various types of wireless gadgets. His property would be under twenty-four-seven video surveillance once they had everything in place.

In the meantime, there wasn't a chance in hell he was leaving his place unguarded.

Which was why he found himself in the town's only hardware store on Main Street at nineteen hundred hours. The same musty combination of smells he remembered as a boy still hovered in the air, and the dust on some of the unsold items had grown by what seemed like inches over the years. The sight of lollipops in a container on the counter did bring a smile to his face, but he wouldn't touch those suckers with a ten-foot pole. A few of those sugar globes had to be older than him.

"Fish weren't biting worth a damn today," Calvin complained, adjusting the cap covering his greying hair. He narrowed his gaze as he formulated the same question as everyone else had on their tongues thus far. "Do the police know who broke into your house again?"

"No, not yet. But you're the first to say *again*, interestingly enough." Lance gestured toward the electrical wiring he'd set on the counter, along with a long list of items he'd need in the coming days. He'd already hit the ATM across the street, due to the fact that Calvin's business only dealt with cash on the barrelhead. "I remember a time when nothing bad ever happened in Blyth Lake. Now? Hell, the place is a den of iniquity.

We have a sheriff who doesn't seem to want to get his ass out of his office chair, a missing girl who was never found, and the recently discovered body of a young girl who was murdered eleven years ago and stuffed into a wall. Add in Deputy Wallace's callous murder and the fact that someone was using the Fetter house as either a place to store some sick mementos of his intended victims or a ruse to throw off state law enforcement...and it's basically a free-for-all."

"I heard there was a photograph of Whitney Bell in with that stack of pictures you found out there." Calvin reached for his reading glasses and settled them on his nose before picking up Lance's list. He reviewed the items and nodded, indicating that he could get everything that was included on the small piece of paper. "As far as I know, she's still alive and well. So, it just might be that those pictures don't have anything to do with Sophia Morton's murder or Emma Irwin's disappearance."

Lance rubbed his eyes, trying to extinguish the burning sensation that had taken up residence in his skull. He'd been dealing with people nonstop today, and it didn't help that Brynn had to leave for those interviews she'd previously scheduled. Worst yet was the fact that Byron Warner had been the one to give her a ride back into town, though that predated Lance's recent efforts to set a few things straight.

In only three days, Brynn had managed to lasso his emotions, bringing him to the point where he wanted to continue where they left off all those years ago. Walking into Tiny's Cavern that fateful night had all but been a fatal blow to his chest. He equated seeing her as if she were the angelic light at the end of a very long tunnel out of hell...one that he'd traveled for far too long and discovered was much too wide, only to find that she'd been right here all along, exactly where he'd left her at the beginning of his journey. He couldn't even imagine the excruciating heartache he would have experienced had he come home to find her married with children, happy in the arms of another.

"Lance?"

He looked up to find Calvin staring at him over the rims of his reading glasses. He'd been caught woolgathering, but he wasn't about to admit that. He played it off as if he was bored with the conversation. What had they left off talking about again? That's right. Those damned pictures of teenage girls.

"All I know is that no one else is breaking into my house, not without gaining a few pounds of lead for their troubles."

Lance pulled out his wallet and waited for Calvin to ring up the electrical wire. The other items could be paid for when they were ready for pick up.

"Do you even have furniture yet?" Calvin asked, taking the cash and making change. He handed back two dollars and a few cents. "I have an old surplus cot in the back you could borrow."

"I had my things shipped to storage before I realized what my parents had done for all of us kids, but I was able to have the Benson twins deliver a few essentials a couple of hours ago. Together with my dad's old twelve-gauge double barreled coach gun. I should have most of what I'll need." Lance left out that he'd had to pay double the normal rate just to get the Benson delivery to happen, but at least he'd have a bed to sleep in tonight. "I'll at least be comfortable while I wait on that scumbag."

"That's good to hear." Calvin took his time opening a plastic bag. He slipped the boxes of Romex inside before ripping the receipt off the old cash register. He never was a man to rush things, which was probably why he was so enamored with fishing. "How are things going with Brynn?"

Lance could only smile at the question, knowing full well

that Calvin was gathering information for the crew at the diner. It was good to know that some things hadn't changed.

"She's just fine, Calvin." Lance lifted the plastic bag with his merchandise off the counter with a small two finger salute. "As a matter of fact, I'm about to drive over to the Cavern. Are you going that way?"

"Not tonight." Calvin took out the handkerchief he kept in his back pocket, similar to how Lance's dad carried his, and blew into the white material. "I think I'm coming down with something. If you ask me, it's those damned media crews bringing in all their horrible citified viruses from that damn metropolis. That Charlene Winston stopped in the other day and asked to use my pen."

"You have a good night, Calvin. I hope you feel better." Lance wasn't about to get caught up in a discussion about a conspiracy theory regarding the difference between city folk, country folk, and their relatively poor health by comparison. "I'll stop by in a couple days to see how that list is coming along."

Calvin lifted his snot rag in a gesture of farewell as Lance made his way toward the exit. The sun was slowly descending in the sky as he stepped out onto the sidewalk. Out of habit, he looked up and down Main Street to see who was around, who belonged, and who wasn't a local. Nothing unusual stood out, though he was surprised to see Pete Anderson walking down the sidewalk from where the B&B was located at the entrance of town.

"Mr. Anderson," Lance called out, already extending his arm in greeting. The man had aged in the twelve years they'd last seen each other, developing a receding hairline and the need for a pair of glasses. "It's good to see you looking well."

Pete returned Lance's handshake, but it was evident he didn't believe the sentiment.

"I appreciate that, but I don't think any one of these folks around here are glad I'm in town." Pete pushed his glasses farther up the bridge of his nose as he looked past Lance down the street. "I know I haven't lived here in years, but I'm being treated like an outcast. I don't appreciate it. I didn't have anything to do with Sophia Morton being murdered or her body being hidden inside my old house."

It was understandable that Pete was on the defensive.

"Detective Kendrick is doing his best to figure out who killed Sophia. I'm sure once he's figured out who the guilty party is, you'll be free and clear of anyone's suspicions." Lance did wonder why Pete Anderson was still hanging around town. Noah mentioned that the former resident of Blyth Lake had been staying at the B&B for the last six weeks or so. It couldn't be easy being away from his family or his job this long. "Are you walking down to Tiny's Cavern? I'm heading that way if you want a lift."

"No, no," Pete said with a shake of his head. "I appreciate the offer, but I'm meeting Detective Kendrick at the diner. I put together a list for him of people who had access to my home during the time frame in question, but I remembered this morning that I hired an outside contractor to rewire the electricity to the barn. I don't think the electrician had any uncontrolled access to the inside of my house, but every bit of information helps, right? He pulled a drop off the main in the mudroom, but I was there that day."

"Anything helps." Lance recalled Pete Anderson doing most of the renovations himself, but it would be mighty interesting to see the list he'd composed for Detective Kendrick. "You take care and tell your wife I said hello."

Lance fished out the keys to his truck from the front pocket of his jeans as he reminded himself that he wasn't a detective, nor was that list any of his business. Yes, it was in everyone's best interest to flush out whomever it was among them who could do something so horrid and immoral, but there wasn't anything Lance could offer that would assist Detective Kendrick in his investigation. At least, nothing more than he'd already contributed.

It didn't take Lance long to reach the small parking lot to the side of the Cavern. It was a Saturday night, so he wasn't surprised to find that every damned spot was taken. He managed to turn his truck around and exit the gravel lot for a spot down the block and across the street in front of the bakery. It was tight, but he managed to get it done.

He'd texted Brynn updates throughout the day, but it would be nice to see her after their alone time got cut short this morning. Finding out that someone had broken into his house hadn't been the best way to start their day.

Was that the sound of a police siren headed this way?

Lance turned off the engine to his F150 and stepped out of the truck. Sure enough, the distant wail became ever closer until finally a deputy's car turned the corner down by Seventh Street and continued toward him up Main. Deputy Foster was the one driving the vehicle, but that wasn't much of a surprise considering Byron Warner had worked the morning shift.

What the hell had warranted Foster to use his sirens and lights?

More proof came that the call wasn't minor when the front door of Tiny's Cavern slammed opened to reveal Charlene Winston and her cameraman rushing down the sidewalk toward their van. It was less than thirty seconds later that two other men vacated the premises in the same manner.

That couldn't be good. Something bad must have happened.

Lance quickly made his way inside the Cavern, seeking out

Brynn at the bar. She was deep in conversation with Miles, Harlan, and Chester. Her blonde hair was pulled back at the nape of her neck where she was trying to rub the tension away that had settled into her muscles.

"Brynn?" Lance nodded at the men, though it suddenly occurred to him that someone wasn't in the usual crowd at the bar. Where was Jeremy? Shit. "What's going on?"

"It's Whitney." Brynn took a deep steadying breath before she dropped the bomb. "She's gone missing."

CHAPTER FIFTEEN

"**I**S THERE ANYTHING left that needs to be done?"

Brynn would have named at least a dozen other chores if it meant delaying the inevitable. She wasn't ready to be alone after tonight's events. Still, she told Lance the truth.

"No, I think that's it for now." Brynn left the softer lights on overhead the counter of the bar like she did every night before walking around to join Lance. His gaze had been drawn to the back entrance down past where the restrooms and her office were located in the hallway. She didn't like that she questioned whether or not the door was locked. She'd already checked it twice, right? "I appreciate you staying so late, but you really should get back to your place. I know you wanted to stay out there to prevent another break-in. After what's happened recently, that's not such a bad idea."

Brynn didn't question the fact that Lance was properly armed for such a confrontation. She knew he carried a sidearm for close-in-point targets and had borrowed his father's coach gun for area targets out to twenty yards. He'd been in the military for twelve years, was well trained in the practice of using firearms, and certainly had the tactical ground fighting skills necessary to handle himself in such situations.

"We're past break-ins, though, aren't we?" Lance ran a hand through his short black hair in frustration, shaking his head in self-recrimination. "I feel responsible somehow."

"You're not, and you know better," Brynn argued, fully believing that the discovery of those pictures wouldn't have prevented Whitney's disappearance. "You were seventeen years old when Emma went missing, and not even anywhere around here at the time Sophia was murdered. Deputy Wallace was killed in cold blood while guarding a crime scene, leaving behind a family who loved him. There was nothing you could do about any of that, just as there was nothing you could have done to stop Whitney from being abducted. There's only one person to blame for all of this, and he's the one who took Whitney Bell."

"You're assuming it's a man." Lance finally gave Brynn his attention. "Something tells me you're right about that, but we shouldn't assume anything until we have more facts in the case. Noah called me a bit ago and said that the police are canvassing the surrounding area, but they are asking that the residents stay close to home."

"Did Noah say why the law enforcement agencies don't want the additional help? I would think Detective Kendrick would take all the assistance he could get."

Sheriff Percy was currently on suspension, and word had it that he was about to turn in his resignation. That left only three local deputies on the payroll. The town was shorthanded as far as their law enforcement officers went, so she found it strange that such a mandate regarding help wouldn't be issued. Blyth Lake was a small community where everyone watched out for everyone else, regardless of hard feelings or feuds passed down from one generation to the next.

"I heard from Harlan there were blood stains found inside the Bell residence that indicated Whitney was in some type of altercation. He and Miles drove to Jeremy's house to see if he needed anything. It was by sheer happenstance that Jeremy decided to go home after eating at the diner instead of coming straight here. Poor guy." Lance shook his head at the chain of events. He then went down the road she'd already tried to block off in her mind. "Whitney's photograph was in that stack of pictures, Brynn. What if whoever took them is going back for the ones who either got away or this sick fuck never had a chance to take?"

"Did you recognize anyone else?" Brynn was almost afraid of his answer, because she'd been at that year's summer camp, as well as Emma, Sophia, and Whitney. "Maybe Detective Kendrick will provide them with twenty-four-seven protection."

"I don't think there was anyone else included who we knew, but Sophia's body being found has obviously set this guy off. This son of a bitch seems focused on Blyth Lake, which is why I'd feel better if you were to come home with me tonight."

"What?" Brynn hadn't meant to blurt out the question as if she'd been offended by his request. She tried to cover her surprise. There was no indication that she was in harm's way. "No, no, no. I'm good here, and besides, my picture wasn't included in that tin box you found. I have nothing to worry about. I can take care of myself, you know."

Right? Brynn hadn't once been frightened about her wellbeing in regard to whoever had killed Sophia. There had been no reason for her to fear someone who was partial to teenage girls. Now that a full-grown woman had been taken, Brynn was second guessing herself.

Lance surprised her when he stepped forward and took her into his arms. She instinctively stepped into his embrace, regretting her response almost immediately. Being with him now made it seem as if all those years they'd been apart hadn't existed at all.

But they did. He'd caused her a great deal of loneliness and pain.

They were different people than the teenagers they'd been in high school. She'd always had confidence in the life she'd planned for herself, and even more so now that the bar was her own to operate. Blyth Lake had always been her home, Tiny and Rose were her family, and the residents were just an extension of that relationship.

Lance coming back as if he'd never left was playing hell on her psyche.

Couldn't he see that they couldn't just pick up where they left off?

They couldn't simply fall back into love, could they?

"This isn't the homecoming I was expecting when I drove into town earlier this week. Everyone is looking at everyone else with suspicion, tensions are high, and unfounded conclusions are being drawn against completely innocent people," Lance murmured against her hair, his right hand stroking her back while his left held her close. "I heard what you threatened to do to Charlene Winston if she wrote an article about my family. It's nice to know you still have my six, blondie."

Brynn couldn't help but smile as she rested her cheek against his chest, but her grin slowly faded. She'd always had his back, just as she fully believed he had hers in an abstract sense.

"Lance, we have nothing to do with this investigation," Brynn pressed, though she wasn't willing to give up this comfort just yet. The last two months had brought up some very emotional memories. She recalled how he'd held onto her back then, too. "The only thing we can do is offer our moral support to Jeremy, just as we did with the Irwins back when Emma disappeared. I'm completely safe here. Honest."

"Like it or not, I became part of the investigation the moment my brother found that body. I trust that Detective Kendrick can do his job, but that doesn't mean we can't take precautions. Whitney was taken right out of her father's house, from what I'm hearing. I don't think I can go back to my place knowing full well you're here all alone." Lance pressed a kiss to the top of her head before pulling far enough away that he was able to take her face into the palms of his hands. "My living room and bedroom furniture were delivered to the house this afternoon. You can take my bed while I sleep on the couch, but at least you'll be close so I don't have to worry about you tonight. You don't want to be the reason I'm sleep deprived, do you? What if I electrocute myself doing the rewiring of my basement? Who would know for at least a week?"

Leave it to Lance to lay guilt at her feet over something she had every confidence wouldn't happen even if he'd gone three days without sleep. The problem was looking into those warm blue eyes and turning down the offer of his bed. Did he really think that the two of them together—alone—under the same roof was a good idea while they were reestablishing a fledgling relationship as friends?

She came very close to saying that she was the one who would need to worry about electricity, but she managed to paste a sweet smile on her face as she slowly stepped away.

They were both grown adults.

Brynn had proven that she had her head on her shoulders and could make sound decisions all on her own.

There was no reason she shouldn't sleep in her own bed tonight. Why then, after going through such a relatively rational checklist, did a reply the total opposite of what her mind had composed come off her lips?

"Let me grab a change of clothes and some personal items."

LANCE DIDN'T BOTHER to suppress his groan as he shifted

awkwardly on the couch cushions, trying his best to find a comfortable position that would lull him to sleep.

He had zero luck in that department and wondered what the hell he'd been drinking when he'd bought this damn leather living room set in the first place. It might look nice, but this crap was uncomfortable as hell. Granted, he'd had the same stupid furniture for close to six or seven years and the leather did wear well. That wasn't going to stop him from driving into the city in the near future and hitting up one of those all-inclusive furniture stores for a microfiber living room set or maybe a La-Z-Boy that he could take a snooze in. This junk was getting relegated to the basement. He had a specific taste he'd grown into, and it wouldn't take long for him to choose the correct furniture.

He and his dad would design and create the wooden pieces anyway, so all he really needed were couches and chairs to complement the warm earth-tone autumn color scheme floating around in his mind.

There were other things he was definitely thinking about—or a specific someone who was currently upstairs lying in his king-sized bed—but designing his house was a safer concept to contemplate at the moment.

The sound of something or someone banging into something reverberated through the house, followed by string of muffled high-pitched curse words. He couldn't help but smile at her language that would even stun the men he'd served with in the Marines. It was more than apparent she'd picked up some of those interesting combinations while working at the bar, but she was able to embellish them in a manner that suited her personality.

What the hell was she doing awake anyway?

Lance shifted until he was lying flat on his back, listening closely to the sound of her movements. All of those floorboards upstairs needed to be tightened down. From the swish of her subdued footsteps, he gathered she'd made her way into the hallway and was slowly making her way down the stairs.

"Okay," Brynn exclaimed as she announced herself in the doorway with a bit of frustration. The moonlight streaming in through the windows cast a beam on her white t-shirt and lime green shorts, highlighting her feminine shape that had filled out nicely since their high school years. The maturity only made her more attractive, and he had to clench his hands into fists to prevent himself from reaching for her. "Did you know that the large oak tree out back needs to be trimmed? There are a few branches that keep hitting the window. Seriously, I'm surprised the glass hasn't cracked yet. It's impossible to sleep here. It's going on five o'clock in the morning and nothing has happened, so I suggest we climb into your truck and head back into town. You can crash at my place. At least there, the ghost of Christmas past isn't knocking on the side of the house."

"Driving back into town would only cut into our sleep time, and as it stands, we're only slated to get four hours at best. I have a delivery of hardwood flooring scheduled at zero nine hundred." Lance shifted onto his side after tossing back the thin blanket he'd grabbed out of one of the boxes that he'd gotten from Dad's place. He patted the cushion, knowing full well she could see his gesture in the moonlight. He'd have to add blinds and curtains to his ever-growing list. "Come here, blondie."

Brynn crossed her arms and stood her ground. She'd piled her blonde hair on top of her head in some type of scrunchy. He recalled she was constantly losing them back in the day. He also remembered taking them out quite often and launching them across the bench seat of his truck while they were tangled together in a moment of passion.

"Do you remember the pact we made about always being

honest with one another?"

Where was she going with this? Brynn had stayed far away from mentioning the night they'd each brought up their plans for the future. It had been one of the toughest, stripped-down emotionally conversations he'd ever had in his life. He'd bared his soul to her, and she to him. In the end, they'd still taken their own separate paths.

"Yeah," Lance murmured, leaning up on his elbow and resting his head in his hand. "I do."

Lance hadn't been sure which direction she was taking this conversation, but he should have known she'd thrash him around until he got whiplash.

It was part of the reason he still loved her.

"We both know we're having sex if I crawl onto that couch with you," Brynn stated matter-of-factly, though she almost sounded out of breath by the time she'd finished her proclamation. "Are you ready for that and what comes with it?"

CHAPTER SIXTEEN

THE INCESSANT KNOCKING didn't ease up until after Brynn reached for her summer robe, still not totally dry from her shower. The silky material immediately soaked up the water drops, clinging to her like a second skin. She was still chilled by the much-needed cold shower.

She hadn't joined Lance on his couch the way they'd both wanted her to early this morning. Instead, she made the sound decision to grab his keys and drive back to town. She'd called out over her shoulder that she'd pick him up around ten o'clock after the delivery of his new living room floor and before she had to open the bar for the day. She hadn't given him a chance to stop her, either.

Brynn had needed her sleep, and she'd made the wisest decision she could under the circumstances. It had nothing to do with the irresistible temptation to join him on his couch.

Right?

The damn knocking started up again.

"Hold on," Brynn called out, figuring it was Julie stopping by to give her an update on Whitney's disappearance.

Brynn had actually driven past Calvin on her way home, both of them slowing down and stopping in the middle of the road to talk to one another through their rolled down windows. She thought he'd been driving toward the lake to fish, but he'd been on his way to talk to Rose and Tiny about Jeremy. He'd been taken to the hospital by ambulance after the stress had become too much on his heart. "I'm coming. Don't get your panties in a wad."

Brynn flipped the deadbolt and swung the door open.

"Sorry about that, but I was in the—"

Lance Kendall stood on her threshold looking as pissed off as the time he'd jumped off the pier at the lake and lost his swim trunks.

"You stole my truck and left me with no transportation," Lance exclaimed through clenched teeth, advancing and forcing her to back up a step. She tightened the sash around her robe with trembling fingers, sensing the passion radiating underneath all his frustration. "You left your cell phone at my house, so I had no way to contact you or to see if you made it home alright."

"You could have called the bar," Brynn replied rather weakly upon realizing that heading into town had been somewhat of a rash decision on her part. She truly couldn't justify her choice without coming across as callous, but she tried anyway. In her defense, though, she hardly ever used her cell phone. She preferred to talk to people in person, if possible. Shoot, everyone always knew where to find her. "Lance, it was five o'clock in the morning and I was running on zero sleep. We'd already established that my picture wasn't included in that stack of photographs you found at your place, so it's a bit of a stretch to believe I'd be some sort of target for this lunatic who just abducted another woman who was in the deck."

Lance slammed the door closed behind him. From the fury lighting the blue flames within his eyes, she was doubtful he'd heard a word she'd said.

"For my own insurance, I took the sawed-off shotgun from behind the bar and brought it upstairs with me." Brynn figured that was a compromise that even he couldn't argue with, but that didn't stall his advance. The back of her legs came up against her cream overstuffed chair that matched the rest of her living room furniture. See? They would have been a hell of a lot more comfortable here. "I wouldn't have returned home if I thought for one second that it wasn't safe."

"The only reason I didn't run the mile here was because Calvin called to tell me that you'd made it home without a scratch."

Brynn had wondered why Calvin had turned around behind her and followed her back into town. She thought he'd forgotten something from home, but in actuality, he'd been seeing her safely home. She would have explained to Lance that those actions alone were the reason she felt safe enough to return to her apartment, but he surprised her when he took her firmly by the shoulders and pressed his forehead against hers and drew in a deep breath.

"Detective Kendrick called me when I was throwing on my jeans to come after you," Lance explained, his gaze searching hers for some reason she couldn't name. She wrapped her fingers around his wrists for some semblance of support as she braced herself for the news he was about to impart. "My prints were the only ones on those photographs. Not even smudges from any older prints. Nothing but mine."

"There's more," Brynn whispered in concern, looking for the answers written on his features. She finally understood why he was angry about her leaving this morning. Some kind of evidence must have come to light that worried him. "I can see it in your eyes. Tell me."

Lance exhaled slowly, acting as if touching her was enough to settle his nerves, but it clearly wasn't nearly sufficient in the grand scheme of things. He pulled her close, turning them so that he was the one leaning up against the chair. He held her tightly against him with his lips now pressed against her forehead.

"I never thought to turn the pictures over," Lance admitted after he'd rested his chin on her head. They'd fallen into an older intimacy that she'd thought had long ago faded, but being in his arms gave her a peace she hadn't felt in years. It was as if everything happening outside this building couldn't touch her anymore nor dull her belief in what this town represented to them. "There were dates written on the backs of the photographs."

Brynn squeezed her eyes tightly shut, wishing she could block out what Lance was about to share with her.

"The date on Sophia's picture was within the coroner's estimated timeframe of her death."

"Was there a date on Emma's photograph?"

Brynn held her breath as she squeezed Lance a little tighter around the waist. She wrapped her right hand around her left wrist, gripping hard as she braced herself for the truth.

"The same date she went missing."

Brynn bit down on her lip to prevent the lone sob from escaping her lips, having cried for her friend over and over again throughout the years. She realized now that her tears had never altered the outcome.

"There's more."

Brynn pulled away, wiping the moisture from her cheeks that had somehow managed to fall from her eyes. She shook her head in denial, wishing he'd just stop talking and destroying her faith in their neighbors and friends. He was basically telling her that someone they had known and trusted had committed vicious and terrible acts against his own neighbors. Who else would have had access to the properties around Blyth Lake, known where to go, and how to hide among them?

There was one way to stop Lance from making this situation worse with each word that fell from his lips…and she followed through with the picture that had manifested itself inside her mind.

And she did so without thinking.

She lifted her heels and stood on her tiptoes…and kissed him with as much passion as her body and soul could muster.

He tasted of cinnamon rolls and coffee, a unique flavor that she'd decided she could never get enough of in her lifetime. She didn't hesitate when she lifted one leg to the side of him, knowing exactly what she wanted from him. She fell into him when he recognized her inherent need and wrapped one hand around her thigh. He lifted her up effortlessly so that both of her knees rested against the back of the chair.

"Oh!"

Brynn gasped as the intense sensation of her mound pressed against the buckle of his leather belt. She'd made herself vulnerable in this position, but her body was on fire. She wouldn't have it any other way as she molded herself to his muscular frame.

She used her tongue to play with his, wanting more of his distinctive taste. The thin robe she was wearing allowed his radiant heat to penetrate every pore on her body. Whatever water drops remained from her shower evaporated into the air in the form of steam.

"I thought you wanted to take this a bit slower, blondie," Lance murmured, slipping his fingers into her wet strands and pulling her head back so that he could have access to her neck. He left a trail of kisses down the sensitive cord before lightly sinking his teeth into her delicate flesh. Arousal broke over her as if he'd taken a hammer to the bell within her. She stopped breathing when he abruptly yanked her hair so that he could meet her gaze. His eyes were aflame. "Tell me you want this. That you want me."

"I've always wanted this," Brynn whispered, tightening her legs around his waist to prove her point. "I need you, Lance Kendall."

Gravity forced Brynn close to his body when he abruptly stood to his full height and began walking through the apartment toward her bed. The explosive passion between them had been simmering below the surface for days, and now they were coming to a boil. She wanted to immerse herself in this over-whelming desire and never come up for air again.

Every part of her body was aching in yearning, and she didn't want to wait a second longer than necessary. Her hands immediately went for his shirt, lifting it up and over his head with his assistance. His blue eyes darkened with longing as she then reached for her sash.

Lance stalled her by taking her wrists and leveraging her forward, securing her arms behind her back. Electricity sparked throughout the bedroom and her nipples hardened against the muscles of his bare chest.

"We need to slow down. This reunion deserves us taking our time."

Lance made an attempt to even out his breathing, but she wasn't going to make it easy for him. They had plenty of time to get to know one another again in an intimate manner, but right now…she needed him inside of her. She needed him filling her. She recalled something she'd done on instinct back in the day that had drawn an animalistic response from him in the cab of his truck over at Lookout Point.

Brynn closed the inch between them and kissed him slowly until he began to respond…and then trapped his lower lip in between her teeth. She bit a little harder before letting him go.

"I want it fast and hard, Lance."

Brynn caught the laughter in her throat as she went flying backward, the soft comforter on the mattress catching her as Lance managed to undress in seconds. She hadn't even had time to get the robe off her shoulders or enjoy the beautiful view of his manhood before he was crawling on top of her and taking her right nipple in his mouth.

Heat blossomed out from her core, shooting electrical current to every erogenous zone ever identified. She arched her body in response and only managed to make herself want him more when his shaft rubbed against her clitoris.

"Oh, my God," Brynn whimpered, sliding her hands through his short hair for some leverage. She ended up sinking her fingers into his shoulders when he kept suckling her nipple until the urge to scream hit the back of her throat. "Lance, please...take me."

Brynn hadn't expected him to break the seal of his mouth on her breast, but it was so worth the short pause in contact when his lips trailed over her ribs and abdomen to ease the throbbing between her legs. Unfortunately, his talented tongue only made the ache that much worse to bear.

How was it possible to forget what this man could do with his mouth? Maybe it was because they'd been younger that she hadn't treasured his aptitude to pleasure a woman, but she certainly appreciated it now that the drought was over.

Brynn had to grab the pillow positioned above her head when he went even lower, nibbling on the sensitive flesh of her inner thigh. He worked his way down to the inside of her knee. By the time he reached the arch of her foot, she'd pretty much worked her way into a frenzied ball of lust.

She certainly didn't expect him to take a hold of each ankle and flip her over onto her stomach, but she used it to her advantage. In a brief moment of clarity, she pointed toward the nightstand.

"Bedside drawer." Brynn closed her eyes to savor his body heat as he rested the front of his chest over her back. His hardened member rested in the crevice of her buttocks, promising her something so much more. She didn't even bother to smother the moan that escaped her lips. "Please hurry."

"You're always in such a rush, blondie," Lance whispered in her ear, triggering goosebumps to scatter over her shoulders. The hair on the back of her neck stood to attention in provocation as he brushed his lips against her ear. "Let's try to slow this down a bit, shall we?"

LANCE WANTED MORE than anything to drive himself inside of her, but he would always put her needs above his own. The snug crevice of her ass was almost too much to resist, but he managed to lean over her and pull open the bedside drawer without sinking himself into her.

Patience was sometimes a virtue.

"Don't you move," Lance all but growled into her ear.

She was in the perfect spot for what he had in mind, but first came protection. He'd always protect her. That would never change, even when she made that task nearly impossible.

Lance didn't waste time. In under thirty seconds, he'd covered himself and tossed the torn foiled package to the floor.

One of his favorite parts of a woman's body was her lower back and the sensual arch that blended in with the curve of her buttocks. He took his time to stroke the hourglass shape of Brynn's back before he brought her fully up on her hands and knees with a gentle tug on her hips.

"Perfection," Lance muttered, caressing her lower back with the tips of his fingers. He let them slide over her butt and continued down the back of her leg. "Fucking perfection."

Brynn's brown eyes met his over her shoulder. He couldn't contain his need for her any longer. He gripped both sides of her hips and eased himself into her inch after inch, causing them both to moan in gratification. The intense gratification was so overwhelming that he had to lean his head back and suck in a breath in an attempt to collect himself.

"I'm not made of glass, Kendall," Brynn said, tossing the words over her shoulder. She was testing his resolve with her exclamation.

"It's not you I'm worried about, blondie."

Lance began to slowly pull out, never once releasing his hold on her. He gradually pulled her back against him, continuing to deliberately take his time in building up to their mutual release. This was the homecoming he'd envisioned without even knowing it...and it couldn't have been sweeter as he gained momentum.

Brynn arched her back as he began to pick up the pace, allowing him to sink even deeper than before. Her wet strands were almost completely dry now and had fallen over her right shoulder as she kept peering back at him with parted lips.

Sexy didn't even begin to describe the look of sheer pleasure that crossed her beautiful features.

"Harder," Brynn whispered in need, letting him know that she was mere strokes away from her release. "Faster."

Lance gave her what she wanted, and he was a goner the moment the first wave of her orgasm triggered her sheath to tighten around his shaft in a stranglehold. He cried out her nickname as he reached the pinnacle of their culmination.

Did she know what kind of power she held over him?

Did she understand that she was the one who'd fired the fatal bullet to his heart?

CHAPTER SEVENTEEN

"I HAVE TO get downstairs," Brynn murmured against Lance's chest, having not one regret that they'd stayed in her bed for another hour. She wasn't even sure how much commitment she had behind the words she'd just spoken. She could easily be talked into allowing Kristen to run the bar for the entire afternoon. "I'm surprised Kristen and Elm haven't arranged to have us SWAT 'knocked yet."

"Kristen pulled into the lot the same time as I did this morning. I came in through the bar, not your private entrance." The temporary pause in the light strokes on her arm told her that Lance heard the second name she uttered. "Wait. Who the hell is Elm?"

"My new cook. And he's a damn good short order guy, so be nice or you'll be the one hitting the road."

Brynn didn't need to issue that warning. In all honesty, Lance was always nice toward strangers. Noah and Mitch tended to cop a bit of an antisocial attitude every now and then, but not Lance. He always gave everyone the benefit of the doubt, with the recent exception of assuming Arthur Fetter's guilt in murdering Sophia Morton. In Lance's defense, he had just found pictures of three potential victims...maybe more.

The town would now have something else to talk about other than Noah finding a young girl's body in his house. Brynn should have been bothered by the fact that their midday rendezvous would be this afternoon's fodder for the gossip mill, but she wasn't ashamed in the least that the townsfolk were well aware she and Lance were getting reacquainted.

Then again, he had mentioned something else had happened with regard to Whitney.

Brynn squeezed her eyes tight and wished they didn't have to face the day with all its uncomfortable details. She wasn't ready for more ugliness, and she certainly didn't want to hear the same words that had been relayed to her the day after Emma had gone missing twelve years ago.

"I like the tattoo," Brynn whispered, buying herself more time as she lifted her lashes to brush her fingers over the letters. The words *Semper Fidelis* were tattooed in script lettering on the left side of his chest, right above his heart. The tattoo was done in black ink, but there was a slight reddish hue surrounding the unique scroll. That wasn't what caught her attention, though. "What happened here?"

Brynn circled her finger around an old scar on his rib cage that was somewhat ragged in appearance.

She was surprised when Lance rolled her over onto her back and leaned up on his elbow so that he could see her expression. He'd caught on to her tactic to delay the inevitable. The softening of his blue eyes was almost her undoing.

"Please don't tell me that they found Whitney's body or anything like that," Brynn whispered, wishing more than anything that they could resume their pillow talk. Why was life always intruding at the worst moments? "Wait. I don't want to talk about something that horrible in a place we made our own oasis."

"Understandable," Lance replied softly, pulling her on top of him and kissing her until everything else faded away. She'd even kicked off the sheet so that she could settle her knees on either side of him. The heat of his torso chased away the coolness that had tried to invade their refuge. "Better?"

"Yes, very," Brynn replied after nipping at his lower lip. The ringing of his cell phone popped the bubble of arousal they'd just begun to form. "Damn it."

"We have to face reality at some point, blondie." Lance kissed her fast and hard before shifting both of them so that they were half off the bed. Her bare feet made contact with the hardwood floor. "I'll make us some coffee."

"Coke. A cold one, too," Brynn practically begged before walking to her armoire. She didn't have a closet, but it wasn't like she had to store two completely separate wardrobes. She didn't have a corporate job and always wore the same basic denim jeans that made her days comfortable, along with shirts she didn't mind spilling a beer on in the course of a shift. That didn't mean she didn't own a nice dress or two for those rare occasions when something more appropriate was required. "With ice, please."

"Demanding, aren't you?" Lance teased from his position on the bed. His hair was ruffled on top in that *I just had fantastic sex* style and his blue eyes screamed satisfaction. It made her want to take the day off and crawl back into bed with him, but that wasn't going to happen today. He must have sensed her change in mood. His smile slipped. "One glass of Coke with ice coming up."

It didn't take long for Brynn to use the restroom and change into a pair of jeans and her favorite pink t-shirt. She always wore it when she was feeling down and out. This was her way of fending off whatever Lance needed to tell her about Whitney.

Sure enough, Lance was in her kitchen wearing nothing but his jeans. Even those were unbuttoned at the top, tempting her once more to forget about her responsibilities. The sight of a cold glass of ice with Coke poured over the cubes gave her the strength to face what was to come. She took a fortifying drink of the caffeine and sugar, steeling herself against the bad news. She waited for the addicting contents to hit her stomach before letting him know with a quick nod that she was ready to hear what he had to say.

"When I spoke with Detective Kendrick this morning, he informed me that another photograph was found on the seat in Whitney's car." Lance brushed her hair away from her cheek. She'd yet to secure it away from her face. It was more than apparent he was using the time to choose his words carefully. "It was a recent picture of Whitney, and yesterday's date was handwritten on the back of the picture."

Brynn almost choked trying to swallow around the sudden constriction in her throat. She was glad she'd taken a drink of caffeine first. It was obvious he was leaving something out from the hedging glance he'd thrown her way, and she wasn't sure she was ready to hear it. She blinked away the moisture that had gathered in her eyes and nodded once again, letting him know she was prepared for the rest of it.

"From what I understand, Whitney wasn't alive in the picture, Brynn. According to the state forensics team's preliminary examination of the photograph, it was more than obvious she was deceased."

The blow from the news was overwhelming. Her chest tightened quite forcefully as she absorbed the news. She couldn't imagine what Jeremy Bell was going through, nor could she fathom the hell Whitney must have dealt with in the facing her imminent death. She hadn't been the nicest woman in Blyth Lake, but no one deserved to die at the hands of a vicious serial killer whom they thought to be their friend. It was as if the act was a double betrayal of the victim's confidence, realizing your trusted neighbor wasn't who you depended on them to be.

"I didn't ask for details from Detective Kendrick, because I doubted he wanted to share them at this point in the investigation." Lance leaned back against the counter and crossed his arms, but not because her apartment was cold. "None of this explains why someone would break into my home, though. It was all over town that forensics had gone through the house with a fine-tooth comb once again."

"It would explain everything if the killer isn't from our town," Brynn said, almost with a sense of relief. It was a conceivable, however slim the chance. Somehow, it was better believing that Whitney hadn't known the person who had taken her life. "Did Detective Kendrick give you any other ideas as to why someone would break into your basement?"

"None that makes any sense to me, if it's at all related to the original case."

"So what now?" Brynn asked, wondering if the state police would now request the help of Blyth Lake's residents. She took another sip of her soda, needing the energy for what the day would bring them. "Do we canvass the wooded areas? Do we put together search parties to try and find her body? We can't leave her out there or wherever the hell he might have…"

Brynn had been going to say the word *dumped*, but she couldn't bring herself to utter the word. It was far too callous.

"Kendrick expressed his desire for the town to go about its normal business." Lance ran a hand down his face in exhaustion. He was running on less sleep than she was, and she was partly responsible. She truly hadn't thought he'd react in such a way to her leaving his place to sleep in her own bed. "So that's what we're going to do. He wants to meet with me and Noah later today, though."

Brynn stepped forward and set her glass down on the counter before wrapping her arms around his waist. They'd just made love, so her support should be evident.

"I'll go with you."

"You mean you'll get my six?" The smile Lance gave her didn't quite meet his eyes. "I'd normally welcome that, blondie, but you have work to do here. Noah and I are meeting him at my place in a couple hours."

"Did Detective Kendrick say why he wanted to meet with you two?"

Brynn didn't like that Lance was still being drawn into an investigation more than he already was in terms of those pictures being in his house. She didn't want either one of them to get too close to whatever evil was circulating this town.

"No," Lance replied, pulling her closer and resting his chin on top of her head. Tension was radiating off his shoulders. She wondered if there was anything she could say to pause time. "But I'm pretty sure it has to do with the fact that two of the most recently purchased houses by the Kendalls are tied to at least one of the murders, a disappearance, and possibly more if those photos mean anything. Honestly, I believe some folks are beginning to think I'm somehow involved in this investigation. The question remains…does Detective Kendrick?"

"Of course he knows that you and Noah aren't involved."

Right? She had to believe that the state police were more competent than Sheriff Percy. Now that man would have thrown any of them under the bus had it meant closing an investigation.

"Lance?" Brynn was uncomfortable with the possible connection that crossed her mind, but she'd been taught by Rose and Tiny that saying a fear out loud took away its power. She didn't want to be right, so she whispered her inquiry and prayed he would deny her train of thought. "You don't think Harlan could be…"

Brynn couldn't finish, because it was a betrayal to verbalize the link she was still denying in her head. She'd known Harlan her whole life, and the man had never done anything to suggest he could do something so horrible to another human being.

"I don't know," Lance hugged her tighter, as if he too had wondered the same thing. "I don't want to believe that anyone we know could have anything to do with those murders and kidnappings, but someone had access to both homes somewhere along the line."

"Miles Schaeffer?" Brynn winced as she tossed out another name. These individuals had been a part of her and Lance's childhoods. "He had access to both homes, didn't he? I remember Miles helping Arthur out a few times around his property."

"Honestly, I think every single resident in Blyth Lake had access to both properties at one time or another. Think about it. I have a pond on the edge of my place that has been known to be the best local site for bluegill fishing for more than twenty years. Noah's barn, pasture, and pond were used by every teenager for years as a hangout and tailgating spot since we were in high school." Lance's sigh was one of frustration and resignation. He kissed the top of her head before pulling away and meeting her gaze with reassurance, though his body language was telling her something entirely different. "I'm sure this meeting is just to go over our limited involvement in making these discoveries and our knowledge of local comings and goings. It'll be fine, blondie. Promise."

Lance pressed a soft kiss to her forehead before stepping away and leaving the kitchen area to grab the rest of his clothes. She picked up her glass of Coke, taking a sip and looking over the rim to enjoy the view. One thing her parents' death and

Emma's disappearance had taught her was to enjoy every precious second life could give her.

Slipping back into their old roles had almost been too easy, but she didn't regret a moment. Brynn had no idea what the future held for them both, and that was okay too. She'd also learned to take her life day by day…one moment at a time.

Why, then, did it feel as if those minutes and hours were limited?

Brynn had gone through that sense of loss in her junior year, knowing that Lance was graduating early and would leave Blyth Lake the instant he had his diploma in hand. Those ticking sounds on the clock had been one of impending doom.

Was it because of Whitney's death? Was it because evil had unknowingly slithered into Blyth Lake years ago, touching each of them in a manner that couldn't easily be dismissed? Or was it simply that being with Lance brought up these pensive emotions?

"Why target the Kendalls?" Brynn muttered, focusing on something other than the fact she'd just opened herself back up to be hurt like she'd done so many years ago. She was getting involved once again with the man who held her heart and had the ability to crush her soul. It had been that way when they were teenagers, and nothing had changed since.

Her gaze dropped to the ice floating in her soft drink. The cubes were helpless against the beverage's carbonation. The process of disintegration was similar to what the town was experiencing in regard to the tragedies that kept unfolding before them.

Hell, look at how easily she'd thrown out names of those residents she'd known her whole life. Hadn't she wondered how long it would be before the townsfolk started to turn on one another? The media wasn't helping, seeing as they were trying to sow seeds of distrust with how the Kendalls were connected to Sophia's murder, along with the pictures found in Lance's home.

Was that why Detective Kendrick wanted to speak with Lance and Noah? Did the state police buy into the hype? Did they believe that the Kendalls were involved? Brynn couldn't shake the ominous feeling that the walls of this investigation were closing in, but she'd be damned if she were going to step aside and allow them to close in on the man she'd just allowed back into her life.

"Lance, I changed my mind," Brynn called out, setting her drink on the counter and heading for the bathroom to make herself more presentable. "I'm going with you to your meeting with Detective Kendrick."

CHAPTER EIGHTEEN

"**L**ET'S JUST SAY that the list of suspects has now somewhat narrowed," Detective Kendrick shared over the coffee that Brynn had made Lance stop for at the diner. She'd gotten herself a Coke to go, but she hadn't take a sip of the soda since they'd parked in front of Lance's house. "But I can't rule out a connection to you and your family. Do I think it's likely? No. Let's face it. Could Noah have *accidentally* stumbled upon Sophia's body due to some kind of guilt you were unable to live with anymore? Sure, though it's highly unlikely. Could you, Lance, have *conveniently* found pictures of several victims to help expose someone's guilt? Maybe, but I don't believe that any more than I believe that crap about your brother."

Kendrick was inferring that the Kendalls, as a family unit, were under attack.

Lance didn't have to set eyes on Brynn to know she'd tensed at the suggestion. This was the reason she was here, because for some reason she didn't like the media or the police making that connection. At least the detective in front of them was willing to see beyond the obvious smokescreen.

They were all currently standing around Lance's kitchen, surrounding the small island that he would eventually remove to make the room larger. This was where the detective wanted to meet, but he'd yet to give his reasons why.

"I bought both of the properties from Harlan Whitmore."

Gus thinned his lips in frustration as he regarded Detective Kendrick with annoyance. "I'm not throwing Whitmore under the bus, and I by no means am inferring that he had something to do with a body being encased inside drywall some eleven years ago. My boys were just teenagers back then. I'd say you can rule out any spurious connections to us."

"I wasn't referring to Sophia Morton," Detective Kendrick pointed out, leveling a look Noah's way. The detective had the appearance of a federal agent, with the square jaw and penetrating gaze. Lance was good at reading people, though, and the man investigating this case was no doubt one of the good guys. He took his job seriously, and he didn't leave any stone unturned. "Deputy Wallace was murdered on your property, Noah. I believe the act was committed because someone was returning to the original crime scene in belief that he left something behind. Do I think the homicide is connected to the fact that a Kendall bought the property? No, but I need to rule it out."

Lance didn't miss the fact that Brynn's gaze immediately landed on him. They'd talked about whether a man or woman had committed these crimes, assuming a male individual was responsible due to a number of reasons. Detective Kendrick must have information if he was so willingly sharing that his suspect was in fact male.

Lance would address his other question about how they could go about ruling out the Kendalls' involvement.

"He?" Lance asked, not blinking twice when he sensed Brynn's hand on his lower back. Noah and Reese were to their left, while his dad and Detective Kendrick stood on the opposite side near the sink. "I take it there is evidence to back that assumption up?"

"Yes, actually, there is," Detective Kendrick shared rather grimly. His brows almost touched as he relayed the forensic evidence that must have come in recently. Lance couldn't help but wonder what other physical evidence had been brought to light. "Sophia Morton's cause of death was manual strangulation. A female assailant is most certainly ruled out from the amount of force used, the tissue damage evident, and the measurement of the indentation left behind by the assailant's hands. I'm sorry, Reese."

Reese leaned into Noah as she struggled to maintain her composure. He'd wrapped his arm around her and tucked her tighter into his body, as if trying to brace her for what might be coming next. It was natural to assume that Sophia had been sexually assaulted from Detective Kendrick's proof that a man was responsible for her death.

It was more than a relief to hear otherwise, but just as disturbing to be told the reason why.

"Sophia wasn't sexually assaulted, but by the width of the killer's fingers and hands, we believe the victim was killed by an adult male individual." Detective Kendrick paused, though it wasn't a hesitation. It was as if he were allowing them to brace themselves for the continuing flow of information. "Although Sophia was wrapped inside a plastic tarp, we found evidence that the killer displayed some level of kindness when *preparing* her body for entombment."

Preparing was a nice way of saying that Sophia was stuffed into a wall and all but forgotten.

"I don't understand," Reese said, after clearing her throat so that her words came out clear. There was no doubting her emotional strength after she'd gone through years of searching for her cousin, and it was clear to see that Noah respected and loved that side of her. She stepped forward and rested her hands on top of the counter. "What do you mean—*kindness?*"

Reese practically spit out the description, her tone letting everyone know she didn't care for Kendrick's assessment of how her cousin was treated.

"Sophia was slowly strangled to death, so how does that horrible scenario even remotely point to this killer showing any amount of *kindness*?"

"Reese has a point," Lance pointed out, sharing a knowing look with Noah. They'd both been in combat and killed to accomplish the mission. There was no kindness shown in death. "Murder is murder. What did he do that was kind?"

"This killer took the time to pose Sophia's body in a peaceful, resting position, with her hands resting over her abdomen holding a flower."

"A flower?" The disgust lining Reese's tone was undeniable. She shook her head to dispel the image, but Lance doubted it would be that easy. "I need some air."

Detective Kendrick waited until Reese had left the room before continuing. It was easy to see Noah struggling to stay to take part in the rest of the conversation when he wanted nothing more than to go outside and comfort Reese.

"This type of behavior by a serial killer denotes that he displays affection toward his victims. I reached out to a friend of mine in the Behavioral Analysis Unit at the FBI. She believes that Emma might have been his first victim, followed nearly a year later by Sophia."

"And you believe we know this individual?" Brynn tightened her fingers so that the fabric of Lance's shirt was caught snug in her grip. "I understand why you would believe all these cases are linked, but you're still saying we would have to know the man responsible. I have trouble accepting that premise."

"Ms. Mercer, it's very rare that we make an arrest in these cases where the neighbors say they saw all the signs of a deranged lunatic. I'm sorry, but these specific individuals are very good at hiding what they truly are on a daily basis." Detective Kendrick reached behind him for the newspaper he'd folded in thirds and set it beside the sink. He dropped it in the middle of the counter so that it opened like a flower, displaying the photograph he'd purposefully intended to show. "You no longer need to worry about who broke into your home, Lance. We know who it was."

There, as big as life, was a photograph of the furnace located in his basement where he'd found the tin can of pictures. Some douchebag thought it was okay to break into someone's home...and all for gaining advantage on his competition. They wanted a picture of where the photos were found.

"An arrest has already been made, but that still doesn't tell us why the killer chose this house to hide his mementos. Lance, I need to ask you a couple of questions about the night you snuck Emma Irwin and Sophia Morton out of summer camp." Now they were getting somewhere. Lance had nothing to hide, and he wanted his involvement in this investigation to be done. Now that he'd been informed that a reporter was to blame for the broken window and illegal entry into his home, he wouldn't need to worry about being targeted by this coward who was preying on women. "You said you were doing the girls a favor for one in return. Ms. Osburn confirmed she met with Sophia, but not Emma on the night in question. We're assuming Emma waited for Sophia outside the diner. What I need to know is whether you saw anyone other than Arthur Fetter that night. Did you pass a vehicle from the lake to town or vice versa? Did anyone visit the camp that week who might have stood out to you? Maybe someone who didn't belong, wasn't dressed right, or was out of place somehow?"

Lance shook his head, having gone over that night a million times since then. The detective obviously wasn't from a small town himself, or he'd realize that almost every adult showed up at camp at some point or another…whether to help out in some capacity or to pick up their children for dinner by the lake. There were visitors at the camp all the time.

"It would probably be easier to tell you who wasn't at camp that year," Lance replied, sharing a look with Brynn. "Birdie owned the property back then. It was her goal to have everyone pitch in as a community, and I'm talking even adults who didn't have children donated their time. She also allowed the parents to visit their kids during their week at camp. Almost everyone's mother and father visited at some point."

"And Harlan Whitmore? You mentioned him a minute ago. Did he ever exhibit any type of behavior that caused you to question his motives or character?"

Silence hung heavy in the air.

Lance understood what the detective meant about neighbors not truly knowing their neighbors, but what he was suggesting just wasn't possible.

"Miles Schaeffer?" Detective Kendrick followed up when he realized no one was willing to take the bait. "I know he had access to Pete Anderson's residence twelve years ago. Do you recall if Mr. Schaeffer helped Arthur Fetter around his property doing small jobs? Mr. Fetter's memory isn't that good anymore. He couldn't recall."

Did that mean the good detective hadn't questioned Miles with regards to his role in this investigation? It wasn't right to be considered a suspect and have no idea he was about to be ambushed, but Lance also understood this was how the cases were solved in the grand scheme of things. Questions were slung around until one of the numerous answers stuck to the wall.

"Harlan and Miles aren't killers." Gus made the statement as if he'd read it from a slab of stone handwritten by God himself.

He reached into the front pocket of his work shirt where he kept a couple of toothpicks and put one in between his thin lips. He wasn't going to hear another word, and that was that. "I think I'll go check on Reese and see how she's doing."

Lance backed away from the island, as did Brynn, giving his dad room to leave the kitchen. Brynn caught Gus' hand from a brief moment, gently squeezing his fingers in understanding. He was friends with both men, and Lance was relatively sure that Kendrick had more suspects on his list than he was willing to say at the moment.

"Murder investigations are never pleasant." Detective Kendrick adjusted his tie, alerting Lance that more information was about to be shared. The man had fiddled with his tie the first day they'd met in person, the night Lance had found the pictures, and now was no different. Noah even straightened his shoulders, as if he'd recognized the small tell the detective displayed when the conversation was about to take a turn for the worse. "Six out of the seven pictures in that tin you found are of missing teenagers from 2005 to 2012. Only one girl was spared, and it appears that oversight was recently corrected."

Detective Kendrick was referring to the killer's point of view, but that didn't make it any easier to hear.

"The other girls…Lance mentioned that he didn't recognize them and they weren't from anywhere around here," Brynn pointed out, setting her Styrofoam cup on the counter. The tip of the straw had been chewed in worry with her teeth. "So wouldn't that mean that you should be looking at someone who travels for their job? Maybe someone who is from another town?"

"Not necessarily. These girls went missing all within a ninety-mile radius." Detective Kendrick zeroed in on Brynn as he continued to answer her question. "A trip into the city or different towns once or twice a year could have been done easily without this individual traveling for his job. What I do believe is that Emma Irwin was his first victim, followed by Sophia Morton. The timeline clearly shows that the suspect waited a year in between abducting his victims. Historically, a serial killer's first victim is someone he actually knows or has associated with at some point in his life."

"So the only one who's been found was Sophia." Noah stepped forward and set his palms on the edge of the counter. "What does that mean?"

"Honestly?" Detective Kendrick thinned his lips in frustration. "I brought that same fact up to my colleague at the BAU. She believes that when he was killing Sophia Morton, he was interrupted in whatever ritual he'd established and had to do something with her body quickly."

"Wouldn't it have been easier to bury the body?" Noah asked in disbelief. "You're asking us to believe that shoving a body into a wall and sealing it inside with drywall was a *quicker* solution?"

"I'm saying Pete Anderson traveled for his job quite a bit, which was known to everyone in town. He took his family with him most of the time. It's not out of the realm of possibility to believe this suspect had knowledge of that fact and used it toward his advantage. When Sophia went missing, the first hard frost had already hit the ground. The dirt would have been rock hard."

Noah and Brynn began talking over one another, with Detective Kendrick fielding question after question. It wasn't long before Reese and Gus came back in from outside and rejoined the conversation. The bottom line was that they were no closer to finding out who was responsible for something so hideous, nor had any of the Kendalls been able to shed any light on the investigation.

Detective Kendrick was still in the dark, though it did appear his suspect list was longer than any of them wished it to be. Many of their friends and neighbors were among the suspects, though there were valid circumstances that supported his reasoning. Kendrick believed someone they all knew had committed multiple murders.

Every piece of evidence was centered right around Blyth Lake.

"Detective?" Lance waited until the conversation died down before asking what no one had brought up this entire afternoon. "What about Whitney Bell? Have you found her body yet?"

"No." Detective Kendrick loosened his tie a little more before meeting Lance's stare. "Which is why I'm having groups of the state's best cadaver dogs canvass the wooded areas around town. We believe this serial murderer has a killing ground somewhere nearby. When we find it, we might just uncover our killer."

CHAPTER NINETEEN

"**B**RYNN, THERE'S NO reason for you not to take some time," Tiny said, his booming voice coming in loud and clear over the phone line. "In case you didn't notice, I sort of miss this place. I don't mind watching the bar for a night or two."

"It's only for tonight," Brynn stressed, not doubting that Tiny was enjoying himself at the Cavern. It was still her responsibility to oversee the day to day operations. "I really appreciate it, Tiny. Is Rose there with you?"

Brynn walked into Lance's kitchen, spotting the different samples of granite that were next to the refrigerator. She honestly hadn't seen them this afternoon. One immediately drew her attention, and it was nice to think of something other than the fact her high school friend was most likely buried some-where...lost to everyone but her murderer.

"Rose is keeping Chester, Harlan, and their wives company this evening. The rest of the usual crowd is here tonight, although Wes showed up around an hour ago. Miles left the minute that boy walked in. Rose's good intentions have definitely backfired." Tiny's pause told her that there was a very specific reason that Rose had joined that group of friends. So much for the reprieve Bryn thought she'd get tonight. She let her fingers slide off the light grey granite as Tiny explained why Rose was compelled to spend her Sunday evening at the bar. "It seems that our friendly detective had a chat with Harlan today. You can understand that he's upset. Also, Pete Anderson finally left town. Irish is here by himself, because Chad was a no-show. I'm assuming he's with Clayton, trying to sort out the family feud. Oh, but your reporter friend is back and circling like a damn vulture."

"Throw her out, if she makes it necessary. She's been given two warnings already. She doesn't get a third pass. Oh, and make sure she knows that I was the one who eighty-sixed her and that she isn't welcome back," Brynn stressed with a bit of frustration. Detective Kendrick had obviously started to put some heat on their friends and neighbors. He'd all but warned them of that this afternoon. Honestly, it was a wonder that anyone was at the Cavern. Had she been accused of a crime as hideous as the ones committed, she'd be holed up inside of her apartment. "I think Lance just pulled in. I'll touch base with you later."

"Okay, baby girl."

Brynn disconnected the line with a heavy heart and walked back into the living room without grabbing the Coke she'd wanted from the fridge. She hadn't missed the fact that Lance had stored a six-pack on the bottom shelf. It was rare that he drank soda at all, so the fact that he'd thought of her when picking up a few items from the grocery store warmed her heart.

She wondered why Lance hadn't come in the door when she'd clearly heard him on the front porch. He'd driven out to his dad's house to grab the rest of his civilian clothes. Had they not been given the reason someone had broken into his house, he never would have left her here on her own. Honestly, she probably wouldn't have wanted to stay here by herself.

As it stood, she'd had some phone calls to make. One of them she wanted to do in private—Shae Irwin. It couldn't be easy having all the details of the worst part of her life brought to the forefront of public scrutiny once again. Brynn wanted to convey that she was here if Shae had any concerns with the way the investigation was being handled. Unfortunately, she didn't answer her cell phone.

Brynn left a message, but all she'd done was request a call back. She hadn't wanted to leave any intimate details on voicemail.

Brynn crossed the old hardwood floor that was in serious need to replacing to the door, gently pulling back the aged curtain. Lance mentioned changing the front door entirely, and Brynn could understand why. It was cracked with dry rot at the bottom and around the window. She was relatively sure it was the same front door the Waltons had on their house.

The porch light was shining bright, but there wasn't a soul to be seen in the front yard. An uneasiness settled into the pit of her stomach. She didn't doubt she'd heard something outside, but it could easily have been a squirrel or some type of little critter scrounging for food. She'd go with that, considering all of Lance's fears about the killer breaking into his house had been unfounded.

The lengths to which the reporters and journalists would go to in order to grab a headline was sickening. Detective Kendrick mentioned that the male reporter had been arrested, though he was saying he'd been provided the photograph of the furnace by an *unnamed source*.

No one believed him for a second.

The picture had been taken with a high-tech expensive digital camera. The same type of camera that the reporter had in plain view on the backseat of his vehicle. The detective was currently waiting on a court order to search the vehicle and camera's video card for evidence of the crime.

Brynn might feel slightly safer that they were aware of who'd broken into Lance's house, but that didn't mean she wouldn't still take precautions. Lance had made sure of it, as well. He'd left her his father's double-barreled shotgun, because that was what she was most familiar with, considering she kept one behind the bar. His had the eighteen inch barrels of a traditional coach gun, but they always said that buckshot was a greater equalizer, especially in a wide pattern.

She'd kept her cell phone with her, so she instinctively pressed the speed dial Lance had programmed into her phone earlier today. The call hadn't even gone through when she caught sight of a raccoon on the far side of the porch.

"Blondie?" Lance answered on the second ring. "Everything okay?"

"Yes." The nickname immediately brought a smile to her face, although it could have been relief at the sight of the inquisitive animal. "You wouldn't want to bring home food, would you? I don't believe those pizza pockets you've got in the freezer are going to cut it."

Brynn made the request for two reasons. She didn't want to worry him with her overactive imagination, and she was really hungry.

"Don't you have good timing? I'm at the intersection of Main, so I'll stop by the diner. Club sandwich and steak fries?"

"And a piece of apple pie," Brynn practically pleaded, finally letting go of the curtain. She walked back the way she came, entering the kitchen and grabbing the Coke she'd wanted earlier out of the refrigerator. "Or peach, if the apple is all gone."

"I'll be home in a bit then."

Brynn slid her phone into the back pocket of her jeans. She popped the tab on the can, her mouth watering at the fizzing sound coming out of the opening.

Home.

This was his home, so why did the word resonate with her? They had yet to really talk about where their relationship was headed, not that she needed to push the issue. They'd agreed to take this day by day. Honestly, it wasn't that hard to do with every other minute reminders that life could be cut short in the blink of an eye.

Brynn wondered if that's what happened with Noah and Reese. She'd only been in town for a little over two months, and that didn't seem to faze them. Their relationship had grown into something monumental in such a short time. The love they shared showed with every look, gesture, and touch. Had they realized how precious time was in the grand scheme of things? Was that why they came together so quickly?

Thud. Thud.

Brynn's stomach dropped at the abrupt sound coming from…where had the noise come from? A raccoon didn't have the bulk to make that kind of racket.

She tilted her head, listening carefully to try and judge the direction or room.

Brynn picked up nothing but silence and the rapid speed at which her heart was beating against her chest. She slowly let out her pent-up breath, setting her can down as quietly as she could on the counter.

Were her senses heightened because of the horrific events these past two months? Was she making something out of nothing? She could admit that her nerves were frayed, which didn't help her current situation.

She carefully and soundlessly made her way back into the living room, her eyes glued to the shotgun in the corner. Her heartbeat steadied, and the slight tremor that had taken up residence in her fingers subsided as she experienced a sense of security the moment her hands wrapped around the blue steel barrels of the firearm.

How was it the air in the house was rather serene now that she held protection close to her side?

Brynn took a brief moment to peer around the curtain of the front door. The raccoon was long gone, and nothing seemed out of the ordinary. She let the stained fabric fall back into place as she made the decision to walk through the house for her own peace of mind.

She decided to start with the upstairs, going from room to room. The more she searched the shadows in every corner, the more she came to appreciate what Gus Kendall saw in this house. It had a beautiful layout, along with gorgeous wood that would no doubt be brought back to life with a coat or two of elbow grease.

Brynn was breathing a little easier when she descended the stairs. She effortlessly cleared the main floor as well. All that was left for her to search was the basement.

Her previous apprehension returned the second her fingers wrapped around the dark doorknob. The metal was colder than the palm of her hand. She never had been a fan of basements, and knowing that a serial killer had been down there at some point to hide photographs didn't help their cause.

Brynn reminded herself that she didn't have anything to worry about. She wasn't included in those pictures Lance had found, and Detective Kendrick had already named the culprit who broke the window and snuck pictures that headlined in this morning's paper.

She steadied her breath and twisted the knob, making sure she stepped back in order to make room should she need to fire her weapon.

There was nothing in front of her but total darkness.

Brynn had no choice but to advance down the stairs. She

flipped the switch and was able to turn on the light above the staircase. She listened closely for any sound that didn't belong in this old house. There was nothing to be heard except for the hum of the refrigerator that had turned on when she'd been upstairs.

She quietly set her bare foot on the first step before slowly descending into what appeared to be the pit of hell. At least, that's what this felt like.

God, she hated basements.

Brynn couldn't shake the visions of a hand reaching through the wooden slats the closer she got to the cement floor. She even leaned down at one point to make sure there was nothing in the back of the basement, but it was too dark for her to make anything out. She'd have to reach the worn string attached to the lone bulb in the ceiling.

"Shit," Brynn breathed as her cell phone rang.

So much for the element of surprise had someone actually been in the basement. She pulled the string and quickly looked around the enclosed area before reaching into her back pocket.

The house was clear.

Lance's name was being displayed across the small screen, so she quickly swiped the button to the right.

"Hey," Brynn answered, doing her best not to sound as if she'd just run a marathon. "Are you on your way home?"

"I'm just leaving the diner," Lance shared, though there wasn't a bit of excitement in his rich voice. Instead, all she could detect was concern. "You're not going to believe this, but I just ran into Tobias Essinger."

"Tobias?" Brynn could easily picture the older man who always had a book in his hand. He was partial to westerns. "I haven't seen him in months. He's definitely not a regular at the Cavern anymore. What happened?"

Brynn turned the light off and carefully made her way back up the stairs. Every door was shut, every window closed, and every lock engaged. There was no one getting inside the house unless someone broke another window. That was a sound she couldn't mistake.

"Tobias asked me about that year we were all at summer camp."

"What about it?" Brynn asked, closing the basement door behind her as she walked into the kitchen. She set the shotgun on the counter and reached for the soda can she'd left near the samples of granite. "I remember that Tobias used to help Birdie out at the camp every now and then, but I couldn't tell you if he was there that year."

"Oh, he was there alright," Lance shared in a manner that had Brynn paying attention. "We began discussing the pictures I'd found at the house. It was as if our conversation triggered a memory or something, because he claims to remember who was taking pictures of us when we were sitting around those nightly campfires."

"Who?" Brynn barely choked out the word, because the name was no doubt of someone they all knew and respected. "Lance, tell me."

"It was Calvin Arlos, Brynn. Tobias was certain of it."

CHAPTER TWENTY

"…ABOUT CALVIN?"

"He was taken in for…"

"…can't imagine…"

Brynn should have turned the jukebox up to drown out the Monday evening crowd. She wasn't sure she could take hearing about Calvin Arlos being questioned by the police for half the night. She sure as hell didn't want to hear the doubt in his friends' voices as each of them came to grips with their own suspicions. Someone mentioned he'd driven into town around four o'clock this morning, which could only mean one of the residents stayed awake to peer out of his or her window.

It wasn't right on any level. These people were neighbors.

Calvin didn't murder or abduct anyone. She refused to accept that. She didn't care that Tobias saw Calvin taking pictures at summer camp that year. The man couldn't even bring himself to go hunting for squirrels, which was why he stuck to fishing year round. How could someone who couldn't gut a rodent do something so horrible to a human being?

And what about benefit of the doubt? Shouldn't Calvin be given some, as well as the town's support?

Brynn didn't like how this investigation was becoming a witch hunt. People she loved and respected were being hurt by their own friends. Who would be next? Rose? Tiny? They were both at camp that year, as were most of the town's residents.

She glanced around the Cavern, uneasy over the absence of regular patrons. She wasn't upset about the lack of business. Quite the contrary. What she wanted more than anything was to be with Lance and his family as they all headed over to Calvin's house to show support, but it was Kristen's night off.

"I don't get a phone call?" Julie quipped, taking Brynn by surprise. She'd been so caught up in her thoughts that she hadn't noticed anyone entering through the front door. "It's a good thing I keep tabs on the gossip column around here."

Julie took a seat on one of the stools, making it glaringly obvious that Jeremy Bell's stool still remained unoccupied. Brynn had signed up for the meal rotation that Rose had started the other day, but her turn wasn't for another two weeks. Everyone was coming out of the woodwork to show Jeremy support in his time of need.

"I'm sorry, Julie," Brynn apologized, reaching across the bar and squeezing her friend's hand. She hadn't meant to cut Julie out of everything that'd been happening, but lately it seemed hard to even have a minute to herself. Not that she was actually complaining. Spending the night with Lance in his bed had the week's events fading away into oblivion. "I should have called. There's no excuse. I'm a crappy friend."

"Well, it's a good thing that I have tonight off so that you can catch me up." Julie set her purse on the stool next to her, taking a quick look around the place. Brynn didn't miss that her friend looked back toward the door as if she were expecting someone. "It's quiet tonight."

"I know." Brynn got to fixing Julie an apple martini, all the while studying Julie. She was once again wearing darker lipstick, along with purposefully putting a few curls in her blonde hair. Maybe her favorite drink would finally get her to talk about who she was trying to impress. Julie deserved to have a little fun, and

Brynn would do whatever was necessary to move that dalliance along. "I'm sure you've already heard, but Lance and I are…well, we're kind of together again."

"Kind of?" Julie lifted the lid to the condiment tray and snagged herself a cherry, as if she'd just popped a bag of popcorn in order to settle back and enjoy a movie. "Details, *blondie*."

"Oh, stop," Brynn laughed, sliding the martini glass across the counter. She had everything back in place behind the bar before allowing herself to continue. Even then, she wasn't sure how to explain how her relationship with Lance had picked up as if no time had passed. "It's like Lance never left, Julie. Being with him…it's just so natural. I'm more *me* when I'm with him. And that doesn't even make sense, does it?"

"Yes, it does." Julie smiled softly and gave a light shrug, as if to say fate would always play out the way it was intended. "I envied what the two of you had, Brynn. You were *the* couple back in the day. You know, the duo who was always meant to be. Don't let time or doubts get in the way of building something together. Make yourself happy."

The way Julie said that last sentence almost sounded as if she were giving herself advice. Brynn studied her friend, taking note of more than just the obvious changes to her lipstick and hair. She seemed brighter, yet worried about something. There was an underlying excitement shining in her eyes, but it was easy to see the doubt she'd mentioned mixed in there as well.

"You said you'd spill if I did, so there's my dishtowel." Brynn waved the bar towel around like she was at a rodeo, not garnering the laugh she wanted to by her antics. It was almost as if Julie was afraid of Brynn's reaction. "Julie, what's going on?"

She would later wish that Julie had fessed up earlier, because maybe then Brynn would have been able to contain her reaction to who walked in the door…and not for a game of darts.

Billy Stanton entered the Cavern as if he owned the place, which was how his whole family felt about all the establishments in Blyth Lake. He came from money—old family money—that had a rooted history here in town. He apparently only had eyes for Julie, considering the way he made a beeline for her at the bar. The thing of it was, he never had eyes for only one woman ever before.

"High school was one thing," Brynn muttered with dread, trying her best to wipe the shock off her face. Julie should know better. "You work with him, Julie. You know how he—"

"That's just it, Brynn. I got to know him. *Really* know him. He's changed, and he's not the insecure tight-end we knew back in high school." Insecure? That wasn't how Brynn would describe Billy Stanton. Julie reached over and rested her hand on Brynn's arm almost desperately in order to catch her attention. It was hard to ignore Billy as he stopped at the last few tables to greet some of the patrons. "It's just a façade. You have no idea what it's like to be Dr. William L. Stanton's son."

"I don't know, but I know Billy enough to realize he doesn't have a shred of common decency." Brynn recalled the day after Emma went missing and how Billy said he'd only danced with her that night because he'd felt sorry for her. He'd stressed that she was nice enough, but she wasn't his type. Neither was Julie, for that matter. Brynn's stomach rolled at the thought of her best friend getting her heart broken over some old crush that could never live up to reality. "You know that, too."

"Did you tell her yet?" Billy asked with a charming smile, resting his hand on Julie's lower back as he leaned in for a kiss. Brynn's stomach revolted, but she'd now had enough time to contain her reaction for her friend's sake. He didn't wait for Julie to answer before explaining how it was they got together in the first place. "Brynn, we never had any intention of getting involved, but being partners for months on end allowed us to get to know one another. We didn't want to get in trouble with our superiors, so we quietly put in a transfer to work with other people. It's also the same reason Julie didn't tell you. Believe me, she wanted to, but it was safer this way. Besides, I've been out of town this past week, so we're only now able to celebrate."

Brynn managed to get the draft beer Billy preferred out of the tap without so much as a drop spilled. She set it down without too much force, congratulating herself on her restraint. She couldn't meet Julie's beseeching gaze. This was the first time that Brynn couldn't support her friend's decision, and it was going to be heartbreaking to watch this whole affair crash and burn.

"I'll leave you two to celebrate," Brynn said with a small smile before gesturing toward the few tables that were full. "Kristen has the night off, so I'm going to go make the rounds."

"Yeah, I'm not surprised it's a light crowd tonight. I heard about Calvin. That's pretty rough." Billy remained standing as he picked up his beer and shook his head with what appeared to be commiseration. Brynn wasn't so sure about the displayed sympathy seeing as she doubted he had any. "I guess it's good for him that the authorities didn't make an arrest, though."

"Calvin didn't murder Sophia Morton, nor did he kidnap Emma or any of those other girls," Brynn replied confidently, unable to stay and have this conversation. What hurt her the most was not being able to support her friend when it was obvious this man made her happy. That much was evident from the way Julie was leaning into him. "I'm sure it was all cleared up last night. If you'll excuse me."

Brynn checked on the two couples playing pool before taking note of what drinks the tables were low on. There were only two older gentlemen at the bar, but they were sitting on the other end. She spent the next fifteen minutes replenishing drinks and putting in one order of wings and another of loaded fries. Unfortunately, the greasy smell wafting from the swinging door behind her wasn't the cause of her nausea.

"I need you."

The brutal honesty with which those words were said sent a shiver of arousal through Brynn's body. Warm lips pressed against her neck as muscular arms wrapped around her waist. The firmness of his body against her back truly made her wish she'd called in Kristen from her day off.

"Hmmm, that's good," Brynn replied in a soft voice, not wanting anyone to overhear them. She was still the owner, after all. That didn't mean she couldn't take a moment to herself. She inhaled his masculine scent as the possibility of closing early crossed her mind. "Because the feeling is quite mutual."

Brynn laughed when Lance spun her around, pressing his forehead against hers. She rested the palms of her hands against his chest and prepared herself for a public kiss. Instead, her smile slowly faded when she caught sight of the worry in his blue eyes.

"Lance?"

Brynn searched his gaze intently, but she couldn't figure out what had happened to cause him so much concern. She was suddenly afraid to ask. Too much had happened these last few months for them to accept another tragedy.

"Calvin had a heart attack, Brynn." Lance shook his head in disbelief, almost as if he couldn't believe he was saying the words. He pulled her close, wrapping his arms tightly around her as if he needed her strength. "He's in intensive care, and they're not sure he's going to make it. He just couldn't take the stress of it all."

CHAPTER TWENTY-ONE

"GEEZ, YOU MAKE more noise when you're trying to be quiet than you do in broad daylight," Lance muttered, not surprised when Brynn's laughter bubbled over in the darkness. He shifted so that she had room to crawl into bed with him. "I thought you were staying at your apartment tonight."

Thursday nights were rather busy at the bar, especially now that things were somewhat returning to normal. Calvin had made it through the first twenty-four hours after having open heart surgery, but his recovery would still be a long process. Lance's dad had driven to the hospital and spent some time with Blyth Lake's resident fisherman. He'd make it through his surgical post-op just fine, but that didn't mean he wouldn't have to make some life changes.

As for things on the investigative front, Detective Kendrick had also taken Miles Schaeffer and Harlan Whitmore into the station for formal questioning. Nothing had come out of either interrogation, but it had effectively shaken up the town. People were second-guessing the relationships they had established with the townsfolk they had known for their entire lives.

"I was going to stay at my apartment, but I heard congratulations were in order. I thought it would be better done in person, though," Brynn whispered seductively, climbing in under the sheet Lance had lifted for her. Her naked form melded into his, and he hardened in reaction. "I can't believe you and your dad didn't stop by the bar to celebrate."

Lance groaned in frustration at the town's ability to spread news as if the apocalypse was upon them. He pulled her on top of him and kissed her thoroughly without answering. Her breasts pressed against his chest, her knees fell on either side of his hips, and the heat from her core foretold him of pleasurable things to come. How did she expect him to do anything else when her touch and subtle fragrance made everything else fade away?

"Congratulations." Brynn was a bit out of breath, so she rested her elbows on the pillow underneath his head. There was enough moonlight coming in the windows that he was able to see her beautiful features clearly. "I know this is what you wanted more than anything."

She'd be wrong on that last account, but that didn't mean Lance wasn't honored to drive up his dad's driveway to find a sign hanging outside the workshop that read *Kendall & Son's Handcrafted Furniture Shop*. It was what he wanted for his future, but it wasn't nearly what he wanted more than anything.

That would currently be the woman lying in his arms.

Lance reached up and gathered her blonde hair, pulling the thick strands over her right shoulder. The cords in her neck were tempting to nibble on, but one taste would lead to hours of lovemaking without having the conversation she wanted in order to hear about the big news.

That didn't mean he couldn't play with his hands in the meantime.

"You'd have to ask Noah, but I'm pretty sure Reese used her phone to videotape me pulling up outside Dad's workshop."

Lance moved the sheet so that it fell below the delicious curve of her buttocks. He then took two fingers on each hand and lightly drew them down her back, not stopping when he reached her arch.

"You were expecting him to ask you, though, right?" Brynn practically moaned that last word as he brought the back of his fingers up to caress the side of her breasts. She reached down and grabbed ahold of his right hand, clutching it underneath her chin. "I wish I could have been there."

"Honestly, I don't think he was expecting me until tomorrow." Lance still had the use of his left hand, which he happily utilized to bring her right leg higher than she had it positioned next to him. This way, he had easier access to her folds. "I'd gone into the city to pick up the painting supplies I needed, plus put in the order for the granite countertops we chose out of those samples."

Lance paused, wondering if she caught the use of the word *we* in that sentence. It was becoming a habit lately, but he didn't mind the implication in the least. It honestly wouldn't surprise him if by the end of the year they'd moved in together.

Whatever was between them started back when they were teenagers, and their connection certainly hadn't been severed by his time in the service.

"What then?" Brynn bowed her head so that her forehead now rested on his shoulder. He continued to use his fingers to pleasure her, sliding them through her center to find her sweet spot slick with her cream. "Did you…"

Brynn's voice trailed off as he began to draw concentric circles around her clitoris.

"I was on the phone with Noah when I decided to stop by Dad's before seeing you, but Noah kept trying to wave me off." Lance smiled when her grip on his wrist loosened, allowing him to shift the two of them so that she was positioned firmly underneath him. He now had full access to her body. "I knew something was in the wind, so I drove straight there."

Brynn's lips parted in pleasure as he slowly slid his middle finger inside of her, taking his time before adding a second. Her heated gaze was focused on his face, though it was hard to see the caramel highlights he loved so much. Her eyes were rather dark with lust in the moonlight.

"Noah must have told Reese that I wasn't listening to a word he said." Lance pressed his thumb on her swollen nub to manipulate the sensitive tissue to add to her rising arousal. "If I'm being honest, it took a few minutes for me to notice that the sign outside my dad's workshop had been switched out for a new one."

Lance began to leisurely and gently thrust two fingers inside of her, loving the snug responsiveness of her sheath. Her breathing had become rather uneven, and her fingers were now clutching the pillow underneath her hair. The slow journey to her release sure as hell was something to watch and would remain etched in his memory.

"I'm sure my shock showed, but I was also overcome with emotion. I know my dad, and he would never have done something so meaningful if he didn't believe I was talented with my hands."

"Oh, you're talented, alright," Brynn managed to say as she arched her back and widened her legs even farther apart than before. "Please stop talking. I don't want to think about your—"

"Only me," Lance whispered, done playing around. He'd given enough information to satisfy her need to know what had happened this evening, but now it was time to satisfy her in another more meaningful way. He curved his fingers so that he was able to stroke that specific area that would have her seeing fireworks. Her scream that followed told him nothing else existed but him. "Think only of me, blondie."

〜

"DID YOU THINK of me today?" Lance asked with a smile, knowing full well it would take Brynn back a week to when she'd crawled into his bed last Thursday. He pulled her down onto his knee, though she wouldn't sit still for long. Now that Calvin was home from the hospital and no new developments had seen the light of day on the investigation, Blyth Lake was slowly returning to its daily routine. At least, it seemed that way. "Seriously, I missed you."

Lance rested a hand on her shoulder and pulled her back so that he could kiss her cheek. She'd turned fast enough to receive his offering on her lips before connecting gazes and shifting so that she was no longer on his knee. She was, however, leaning over him in a way that made him wish they weren't in the bar.

"You'll have to show me later," Brynn whispered into his ear, the warmth of her breath sending arousing shivers to all the right places.

Lance was left alone with his brother, Reese, and a few friends he hadn't seen in years. That didn't stop him from watching Brynn walk away with a graceful sway that had him craving more than a kiss. Apparently, he wasn't the only observant one.

"Shouldn't Warner be at the station?" Lance reached for a peanut out of the bowl in the middle of the table. It was best he cracked the shell instead of the deputy's skull. "Detective Kendrick might be the lead on this investigation on a state level, but Byron still has responsibilities."

"Responsibilities he doesn't want," Noah stressed, most likely accurate in his assessment. "He as much as said so at the town hall meeting, but it's not like he has much of a choice. The department only has one elected sheriff, along with three deputy positions."

"Don't forget Patty," Beth Ann chimed in after finishing off the last of her beer. She pointed the empty bottle in the direction of the station down on Main Street. "She doubles as the dispatcher and the administrative assistant to the sheriff. I swear she's the only person keeping that office afloat right now. I heard that Byron has pushed so much onto her this past month, and that's so unfair. She isn't being paid to do his job."

"Oh, Byron's not that bad," Jack said, appearing rather uncomfortable having this conversation. He was the son of Molly, one of the waitresses at the diner. Had Lance spoken out of turn? He'd been friends with Beth Ann since high school, but he didn't know Jack all that well. The man was older than Mitch by a few years, but rumor had it that Beth Ann was waiting for Jack to propose. "Byron's just in over his head, that's all."

"And you're only saying that because he's your second cousin," Beth Ann clarified with a slight roll of her eyes, confirming that Lance should have kept his mouth shut. "Or is it third cousin, once removed?"

Lance breathed a sigh of relief when Reese smoothed over the conversation, but the topic of discussion somehow veered right back to the fact that it was *her* cousin that had been forgotten in that wall for eleven years.

"You worked the camp that year, Jack. Do you remember anything unusual happening with either Sophia or Emma?"

Lance shared a curious glance with Noah when Jack didn't reply right away, but rather took a long draw on his beer. He set down the bottle and twisted it around until the label was facing toward him. With a smack of his lips, he leaned back in his chair and zeroed his gaze on Beth Ann. She appeared confused, and she wasn't the only one.

"Crap," Noah muttered, causing everyone at the table to see what had caught his attention. The legs of his chair scraped the floor as he stood, motioning for Lance to do the same. "It looks as if we're going to have to step in for Chad."

Lance wasn't ready to let Jack off the hook from whatever he'd been about to say regarding Sophia and Emma, but it wasn't as if he had a choice. A fight was brewing near the bar and everybody was giving Clayton and Wes Schaeffer a wide berth. Chad was usually the peacemaker of the family, but he wasn't around tonight. Neither was Miles, for that matter.

"So much for unity." Lance fell into step behind Noah, allowing his brother to take the lead on this. They shouldn't have to clean up family squabbles, especially between these two Schaeffer boys. "We could always let Warner handle this. Maybe he can do his job for once. Hey, Warner! You want to—"

"...you'd like that, wouldn't you?" Clay practically spit the tail end of his question. He swung his head to the side, taking with it the long strands that hadn't seen scissors in quite some time. His dark gaze narrowed in on his middle sibling. "Well, fuck you! I'll take care of it myself."

Clay abruptly turned, shoving Warner out of the way who'd finally stepped up to the plate. Byron muttered something of a warning, but it most likely fell on deaf ears. Clay stormed out of the bar and left the patrons with something else to talk about than the murder investigation hanging over this town.

"Wes, you alright?"

Wes was shaking his head at his brother's behavior, his eyes glued to the door in what looked to be concern more than anything else. He was also rubbing his chest where Clay had gotten in a good throw in an attempt to make his point...whatever that might have been.

"Yeah," Wes said with a nod and a look of disappointment. He tried to brush off what happened with the typical excuse, but something told Lance it was more than just arguing over the family business. "The usual, you know?"

It didn't take a genius to figure out Clay had somehow heard about the lunch Wes had with his dad today. Everyone in town was aware that it was Clay who'd wanted to break out from underneath their father's thumb. It was the reason he'd started a similar business in the city. Taking Wes had been the icing on the cake.

"Wes, sit," Brynn called out, tapping the counter with a sympathetic hand. Lance figured the man had brought it on himself to be used as a pawn between father and son, but maybe Wes was finally growing a pair. "Calm down and finish your beer."

Everyone began to settle back in place, which was usual after these types of altercations. Normally, it was Tiny's presence alone that kept bar fights from breaking out. With him only here half the time, maybe Brynn should think about getting a bouncer on the weekends.

"I heard your oldest brother is thinking of running for sheriff."

Lance closed his eyes and willed himself some patience before addressing the statement. He wasn't in the right frame of mind to talk to Byron Warner, especially after constantly catching him watching Brynn from afar. The man still had a thing for her, and that could potentially be a problem.

"Oh, you know how it is," Lance began to smooth things over, noticing that Noah had already joined Reese back at the table. He always did manage to leave Lance holding the bag. "I think Dad likes the idea, but Mitch is still processing out. I doubt he's even had time to consider what he wants to do when he gets home."

"Well, Mitch would have my support," Warner replied, surprising Lance with his honesty. To say Mitch was the complete opposite of Percy in every aspect as a man was an understatement. "The department hasn't seen justice done for this town in a lot of years, and I'm just not cut out for the bureaucracy between agencies. I'd rather stick to the job I signed up for and clock out at the end of my shift."

Lance wasn't sure what he could say as a follow-up to that admission. It turned out he didn't have to say a word, because Warner changed the subject to the one that was off limits. At least, from Lance's standpoint.

"Brynn is one of the sweetest women in this town." Warner shifted his weight to his left leg, giving him the leverage he needed to peer around Billy Stanton and Julie Brigham. The blonde was doing her best to bring Brynn into whatever conversation was going on between the couple, but it was a useless endeavor. It just so happened that Warner's description of Brynn told Lance all he needed to know. "It's good to see her happy."

"I appreciate that, Warner," Lance conveyed honestly, though he did need to clarify something. "You should know that Brynn isn't sweet. She's fiercely loyal, has no problem telling someone the brutal truth, and would hunt you down to the ends of the earth if she thought you so much as pulled a strand of hair out of one of her family members' heads. She's not sweet, Warner. But she is mine."

Lance clapped Warner on the shoulder good-naturedly, fully understanding where Byron went wrong in his pursuit of Brynn. Warner was a good enough guy, but not for Brynn. Unfortunately, he had a soft side that triumphed over the part he needed to have in order to manage people in an effective way. His compassion made him a great deputy, but he had none of the leadership skills needed in order to control and direct those underneath him or work his way around the politics of the job.

"No word on finding Whitney's body?" Lance asked, having

caught sight of Jeremy Bell's empty seat.

The man had become such a fixture of this place that no one wanted to disrespect him by sitting in his stool. Somehow, that considerate gesture told everyone just how much the Bells were part of this community, regardless that Jeremy wasn't the most beloved resident in town.

"Detective Kendrick has been giving me updates on the investigation, but he's not having any luck on locating where Whitney might be." Byron shifted his weight on the work boots he hadn't changed out of at the end of his shift, though the gesture and the way he'd said the detective's name hadn't been made out of nervousness. If Lance wasn't mistaken, there was criticism in Warner's tone. "Kendrick doesn't seem to understand that the townsfolk respond better to a kind word than the stick."

Hell, maybe Lance was wrong. Warner could very well learn how to do the sheriff's job if he truly wanted all the responsibilities that came with the position.

"I've got to say, I was surprised myself that Kendrick would pull Calvin and Miles in for questioning, as well as Harlan and a few of the other adults who'd been up at camp that year."

"Kendrick won't get any useful information if he continues down that particular road, that I'm certain of. If anything, the person responsible for killing and abducting those girls for the last twelve years might actually lose whatever control he had over his urges." Warner glanced back at the group he'd been sitting with earlier, holding up his hand to catch their attention. It was clear this conversation had left a bad taste in his mouth. "Listen, I've got to be in the office bright and early. I'm calling it a night. Have a good one."

Lance sought out Brynn, who had already poured Wes a drink. People tended to tell all their troubles to the person with the bottle in their hand. Would Kendrick target Tiny? Bridges had already started to burn, but that didn't mean the whole town should be reduced to ashes.

It was understandable that Kendrick wanted to unnerve the killer into thinking the police were closer than they actually were in terms of an arrest.

But at what cost?

Would the good people of Blyth Lake implode under the pressure?

CHAPTER TWENTY-TWO

BRYNN CUT THE engine to her car, though her headlights remained on and directed toward the left side of Lance's house. She hadn't wanted to sleep alone tonight, not after hearing multiple conversations about Whitney Bell and where the killer might have dumped her body. It had been a godsend when she'd been able to announce last call.

She'd actually gotten out of the Cavern at a decent time, noting that the radio clock read two-forty-eight. Crawling into the security of Lance's warm embrace was exactly what she needed right now, but first she had to find her cell phone that had slipped off the passenger seat when she'd made the turn into the driveway. That would teach her to take the time to run upstairs to her apartment for her purse instead of just grabbing her keys from the office.

"Damn it," Brynn muttered, sliding her hand in between the passenger seat and the console.

She wiggled her fingertips. Her phone wasn't there, which could only mean that it had either fallen underneath the seat or landed on the back floor. She opened the driver's side door and fought the urge to stretch her muscles as she stood, knowing she'd be inside faster if she didn't waste time. The headlights chose that moment to shut off, which was probably why she looked in that direction.

"Lance?"

Brynn couldn't stop his name from escaping her lips even though her brain registered that the man standing a mere twenty feet away wasn't Lance. Her throat seized on the letter C, and her palms became coated with perspiration that didn't have anything to do with the humidity hanging in the air.

The threatening silhouette was positioned in front of the house. The lighting from the porch made it impossible to see the man's features, but that wasn't what put Brynn at a disadvantage. It was the fact that she'd stepped far enough away from her car that she couldn't reach the steering wheel. One press of the horn would have alerted Lance that something was wrong, and he would have come running to her rescue.

As it stood, Brynn doubted she could make it back inside her car without this man reaching her first. She had no cell phone, the path to the house was blocked, and she doubted screaming would penetrate Lance's bedroom windows located at the back of the house.

Neither she nor the intruder moved…yet.

Out of the clear blue, a memory from when she'd driven Rose's vehicle for the first time in high school began to form in Brynn's mind. Tiny was always giving her pieces of advice on how to protect herself. One of them was that ordinary things could be turned into a weapon.

One of those items was a set of keys.

Brynn instinctively shifted the car keys in her hand until one of the serrated edges was secured between her knuckles. Unfortunately, using her newfound weapon would have to be her last resort, because that would mean he would be close enough for her to use it.

Her options were limited, but her fight or flight instinct was kicking in. She had to make a decision soon.

The man made it for her by taking a step forward.

Brynn turned and ran, somehow instinctively knowing he'd reach her in a matter of seconds if she stayed on the driveway. She veered to the left where the reach of the light from the porch faded into the shadows. The darkness finally swallowed her whole, but by then all she could hear was the blood rushing through her eardrums.

She was now at a disadvantage.

It was getting harder to see the path in front of her, and she couldn't make out any sound of his approach. She braved a glance over her shoulder, barely catching sight of his silhouette maybe ten feet away.

He was too close.

There wasn't a chance in hell she was getting away from him, and she'd now distanced herself from the house. Maybe she could double back.

She had no choice but to take him by surprise.

Brynn was grateful she didn't have time to think things through or else she doubted she would have gone ahead with stopping dead in her tracks. She spun around and used all her strength to swing her arm toward his face as if she were going to give him an uppercut to the jaw.

The serrated edge of the key made impact somewhere on the man's face, though he somehow still managed to grab her arm. She unconsciously lifted her leg with all her might, sending him straight to his knees.

Brynn was wearing the t-shirt she'd worn to work behind the bar, so his grip had nothing to hold on to but her bare arm when she twisted away. She stumbled slightly, but she managed to gain footing as she took off at a dead run toward the house. There was no way in hell she was turning around to see if he'd gotten to his feet.

The best thing for her to do was head toward the back of the house, where Lance would be able to hear her. Screaming for help was her best option for several reasons. She couldn't take on the attacker herself due to his size and Lance had a shotgun. Those suckers would put a stop to whatever this intruder wanted to take from the house.

"Lance! Lance!" Brynn didn't care that the man heard her or that her frantic yelling gave away her location. "Help! Lance!"

Brynn had reached the back of the house and finally allowed herself the luxury of looking over her shoulder right before she rounded the corner. Her heart was already beating hard against her chest, but it literally slammed to a stop when she saw how close her pursuer had gotten in his attempt to reach her.

It was then that the front porch light shone brightly on his face, revealing his identity.

Clayton Schaeffer.

His face faded from view as she continued to run around the house, her adrenaline kicking in once more. She never stopped screaming for Lance, even as she passed by the upstairs windows.

Lance had to have heard her, and she didn't doubt that he would be coming out the back door. The light shining from above was like a beacon to her location. Unfortunately, she couldn't take the chance of stopping long enough for him to do so without risking Clayton catching up to her.

Brynn had no choice but to stop screaming long enough to take another breath, having practically no oxygen left in her lungs after yelling, running, and basically trying her best to stay alive. It was then she realized she was no longer being chased. There were no heavy footsteps on the ground behind her, nor did she hear Lance calling back to her.

Silence.

Brynn abruptly stopped, almost tripping over her own two

feet. She was on the other side of the house, putting her in between the back and front yards. Light illuminated from both ends, revealing no one.

Not Clayton Schaeffer.

Not Lance.

The strong smell of gasoline hit her out of nowhere. No wonder the alarm system hadn't been activated.

Clay hadn't been trying to break into the house.

He'd been trying to burn it down.

"I didn't want this."

Brynn had been looking in both directions, not expecting Clayton to come up on her from behind. She spun around and took the stance Tiny had taught her to take should she ever need to fight. Some of her hair had fallen over her eyes, coming loose from the band the moment she'd started running. She whipped her head to the side to clear her view, not daring to lift her hands from their position.

"You don't have to do this," Brynn tried to reason, not wanting this confrontation to become physical. "You can—"

"You weren't supposed to be here," Clayton muttered, almost as if he were talking to himself. He ran a hand through his brown hair in desperation. That was not how she needed him to feel at the moment. "I heard you say you were staying at the bar tonight. You said you'd be staying there. Why aren't you there?"

Clay was starting to ramble, which could only mean he was about to panic. Well, the sight of him pulling a Zippo from his front pocket had her panicking, too.

"You said yourself that you didn't want to do this, Clayton." The smell of gasoline was so strong, she was no doubt standing in it. If he were to light that thing and drop it, she'd be on fire before she could move. "Lance is inside, and I'm standing right here in front of you. We've known each other our whole lives,

Clayton. Whatever you've done is in the past—"

"You think I killed that girl?" Clayton asked in disgust, looking at Brynn as if he didn't know her at all. She'd aggravated him, when that was the last thing she wanted to do. He struck the wheel, igniting the lighter. "That's why I have to burn the house, Brynn. You all think I could actually hurt Emma, Whitney, and those other girls."

"What else are we supposed to think, Clayton?"

Brynn almost stumbled backward at the sound of Lance's voice. He'd heard her scream, and he'd come to her rescue. Unfortunately, Clayton had already lit the Zippo lighter. Its flame was dancing in the early morning breeze as if it didn't have a care in the world.

The shotgun in Lance's hands could take care of the problem in front of them, but Brynn would probably be in flames before Clay hit the ground. Shotguns also threw a lot of sparks from the end of the barrel. It would only take one piece of burning propellant to ignite the fumes rising up from the ground.

She wasn't ready to die.

She wasn't ready to leave Lance behind.

CHAPTER TWENTY-THREE

"I T WASN'T ME, Lance."

Clayton held up the Zippo lighter in warning, though the flame started to wink in the wind. The flames were sure to survive, even if Lance shot him.

It was only a matter of time before Clayton dropped it to the fuel-soaked grass below.

Brynn took a hesitant step backward, closer to Lance.

Good girl.

Lance had woken out of a dead sleep the second he'd heard his name being screamed through the windows of his bedroom. Being a light sleeper was a habit from his time in a combat zone. He'd never been more thankful for that training than he was at this moment.

"I'm going to give you one chance to snuff out that flame, Clay. I've already called Patty at the station. It's over." Lance held the shotgun close to his shoulder. There was something very vital that this man in front of him needed to know. "So I'm going to make this simple—if you drop that lighter, I'm going to cut you in half with this double-barreled twelve-gauge."

Brynn was muttering for Lance to stop where he was so that he didn't step on the saturated grass next to the house.

That wasn't happening.

They were in this together.

He didn't stop walking until he was by her side.

"I'm not going to hurt either of you," Clay practically screamed, his frustration at their lack of understanding coming through loud and clear. "Just move. That's all I'm asking. I'll go down for arson, but I'm not going down for some bullshit murder rap."

Lance rested his finger on the trigger, more than willing to shoot the son of a bitch who might hurt Brynn. Her hand was bleeding, but then again, so was Clayton's face. Some type of altercation had taken place, and that alone was unacceptable.

Throw in the fact that Clayton wanted to burn a perfectly good house to the ground, and that was a recipe to land his ass in jail for a very long time.

If he didn't die first.

"I'm not moving, Clay. So if you drop that lighter, you will be committing murder." Lance wasn't willing for Brynn to give her life, so he talked to her underneath his breath. "Run."

He'd always known that Brynn was stubborn, fierce, and downright loyal to a fault. Those were only some of the qualities he loved about her, but they might very well be the reason she died here tonight.

"Listen to me for once."

"Damn it, Lance," Clay called out, past the point of frustration. "Don't you get it yet? I was at the Anderson house when they were putting in that wall. Detective Kendrick already questioned me, my brothers, and my dad. It's only a matter of time before the police figure out that the mark on the basement stairs in your house was left by me."

Clay put a fist to his mouth, as if he were trying to keep it together. The flame was still flickering away behind its perforated shield. Lance braced himself to make his move, knowing full well this was the only chance he'd get if he couldn't talk Clay down from whatever ledge he'd walked out onto in his hazy panic.

"Move." Clay's directive came out strangled. Lance's stomach tightened to the point of pain when he could only stand there and watch as a man he'd grown up with threaten to harm the lives of two people. "Please."

"We're not moving out of your way, Clay," Brynn said softly, almost with an understanding tone. What the hell was she doing? She could have easily made it to her vehicle by now, but instead, she was trying to rationalize with a man who'd poured gasoline around Lance's house and currently had a lit Zippo in his trembling hand. "If you say you didn't murder Sophia or take any of those women, we believe you."

"The cops won't, and you damn well know it." Clay rested his hand on top of his head, grabbing ahold of his hair and practically pulling the strands out in chunks. "They're doing whatever they can to tie this to one person. Look at Calvin. The man took pictures of those girls for Birdie's scrapbook, but that fucking detective tried to twist it into something it wasn't. And what about Harlan? He's the one who sold off those properties…then and now. They dragged his ass into that interrogation room, too. I'm next, and when they find out that I was having sex with Whitney…it's all over."

Lance figured Clay was right. Unfortunately, not about being accused of murder. The fluid in the lighter was dwindling. They all had mere seconds before Clay either dropped it to the ground or made the wise decision to douse the wavering flame.

"Clay, I've spoken to Detective Kendrick." Brynn took a step forward, pulling away when Lance tried to stop her. "He's not like Sheriff Percy. Kendrick will listen to what you have to say. He won't make any rash judgements. I promise you, Clay. Just please…please do the right thing here."

Brynn's faith in this town was unwavering. Her devotion to

the residents even more so, despite the fact that their fate currently rested in the hands of an unstable neighbor. Clay had been pushed to the brink, and not even his family had been able to get him to see reason. It didn't take a genius to figure out this was what Clayton and Wes had been arguing about at the bar.

Lance raised the shotgun, never altering his breathing or taking his gaze off the flame. In his mind's eye, he'd pull the trigger the moment Clay released the lighter. It would take mere seconds for the licking flames to reach Lance's boots. The chances of him reaching Brynn and throwing her to safety were nil, but that's what he would attempt nonetheless.

He couldn't allow her life to end.

He wouldn't.

Lance applied pressure to the trigger. If this were his last action here on earth, then by God, his family would know who was responsible for his death.

"Damn it!" Clay flicked his wrist until the lid closed on the lighter, extinguishing the chance of them all looking like burnt Sunday roasts. Anger and despair were written across his features, and he was glaring at them as if him chickening out of what he'd come here to do was all their fault. "I'm fucked, Brynn. Can't you see that?"

Brynn didn't answer. Instead, she spun around and took the few steps needed to be in Lance's embrace. He could literally feel the sob of relief wrack her body. Anger consumed him at what she'd been through this evening, but he forced himself to lower his weapon. He wouldn't do what had become instinct, thereby removing the threat in front of him.

Lance was no longer on the battlefield, but it seemed as if war had been declared on the residents of Blyth Lake. He had no choice but to take up his trained position once again.

Sirens broke through the silence, only there was no justice to be had this evening. At least, not for the missing girls.

CHAPTER TWENTY-FOUR

DEPUTY FOSTER HAD arrived first, followed by Byron Warner and then eventually Detective Kendrick. An ambulance and the men from the volunteer fire department also pulled up within ten minutes from Foster placing calls to the right departments. It wasn't a surprise to see Gus, Noah, and Reese walking up the drive, right along with Rose and Tiny.

Hell, they might have the entire town show up in another twenty minutes.

"You'd think we were hosting a town gala," Brynn jested gently, wishing she could elicit a bit of laughter from Lance. They were sitting on the tailgate of his truck, with her tucked in underneath his arm and both of them watching the chaos around them. He hadn't left her side, though he was still glaring Clay's way. "Lance, he's just scared."

"He let fear overcome his better judgment, and we could have died as a result."

Lights were flashing in the driveway, making it seem as if Christmas had arrived early. In a way, it had. Clayton made a life-altering decision that had left all of them still breathing. That was saying something, right?

"What the hell happened here?" Noah asked, his eyes darting from Lance to her numerous times before landing on his brother.

Gus was right by Noah's side, though Reese had turned

around and placed her palms on the tailgate to hoist herself up. She stroked Brynn's arm in comfort.

"Are the two of you alright?" Reese asked softly, her dark gaze settling on Brynn's right hand that was covered with blood.

"It's not mine," Brynn reassured her, figuring that's what everyone thought. Tiny moved Noah out of the way with just his presence, making room for Rose to stand in front of Brynn. "I'm okay. Really. I remembered what you said about making ordinary items into weapons. I used my car keys just like you taught me."

"That's my girl," Tiny said in praise, though his features were set in stone. Brynn recognized that look from when he had to kick the riffraff out of the Cavern. She attempted to grab his arm to stop him from making a mistake, but it was too late. Tiny had already spotted the culprit being put into the back of Kendrick's vehicle. "Schaeffer!"

"Let him go," Lance murmured, pulling her closer. "It'll do Kendrick good having to deal with a pissed-off father, because he hasn't seen anything yet."

"We warned him this would happen." Gus reached into the lone pocket on the front of his shirt, pulling out one of those trusty toothpicks of his. Brynn realized early on that chewing on them relived some of his tension. Lance could learn a thing or two from his father. "Kendrick can't go rounding up good people and making everyone think they're a suspect. He needs more than circumstantial evidence before he drags people off to be questioned."

"Is that what happened here?" Noah asked, watching as the rest of the Schaeffer boys came marching up the driveway. "Clayton thought he was going to be arrested? Why?"

"Clay must have been the one to work on the basement stairs," Lance surmised accurately from what Clayton had told them earlier. Brynn could relate to the fear that must have run through him when he realized that all the evidence was pointing directly at him. "He mentioned putting some sort of mark in the wood, saying that Kendrick would assume he was the one who had free access to this house. He'd already been questioned about the Andersons' place. Clayton poured gasoline around the house and was about to torch it when Brynn came home from the bar."

"I think Whitney going missing and then being declared dead by the police might have sent him over the edge, though." Brynn looked up at Lance, seeing him nod in concession. "He and Whitney were apparently…"

"Having sex?" Rose asked, raising her eyebrow as she finished Brynn's sentence. "That doesn't surprise me. He and Whitney used to sneak off to Lookout Point every so many weeks back when they were teenagers."

"I'm sorry, what did you say?" Detective Kendrick interrupted, having brought Tiny back to where he couldn't get near Clayton. He made it a point to look everyone in the eye before turning his full attention to Rose. His displeasure was evident. "Mr. Schaeffer came clean to me about meeting up with Whitney last month, but he didn't mention anything about being in a long-standing relationship with her."

"Oh, you misunderstand me," Rose corrected with a wave of her hand. Kendrick moved his suit jacket to the side, setting his fist on his hip. He was struggling for patience, but Brynn agreed with Gus at this point. He'd been warned about the close-knit community. "Clayton and Whitney never dated formally. They were just…"

"Friends with benefits?" Reese offered up, casting a suspicious glance in Clay's direction. "Did he ever come into contact with Sophia?"

"Clay helped out around the camp, just as many of the townsfolk did back then." Rose patted Tiny's hand when he rested his palm on her shoulder. "But if you're asking me if I saw something unusual, I didn't see him do anything suspicious. Detective, we've been over this numerous times and—"

"Which is why I'm surprised I'm hearing something new at this point," Detective Kendrick pointed out, running a hand of frustration down his face. "Lance and Brynn, I'd ask to speak to the two of you in private, but I somehow doubt that's going to happen tonight."

Brynn surveyed their family standing around the back of Lance's pickup truck. No one even contemplated moving from their spots. They had all gathered around to show their support, much like Miles and Wes had done for Clayton. Chad was missing, which spoke volumes about his troubled relationship with his brother.

"We can get Clay for attempted arson and assault, as well as—"

"No," Brynn exclaimed, shifting her body so that she could hold tight to Lance's hand. Couldn't he see that pressing charges wasn't the right thing to do? "Clay was scared. You know he wasn't going to hurt us. I suspect he never would have gone through with any of it."

"And what if Clay had dropped that lighter by accident? What if you hadn't been here to dissuade him?" Lance asked, shaking his head in disbelief. Brynn figured he was more frustrated over the fact that Clay had put all of them in this position to begin with. "We'd both be dead. Or at least, I would be. I'm not even talking about the fact that he was going to burn down my house."

"He thought he was going to go to prison for a crime he didn't commit."

"Are we sure he *wasn't* involved?"

Lance was angry, and she understood why. But that didn't mean they couldn't show compassion toward someone they'd known their entire lives.

"Can you honestly sit here and tell me you truly believe Clayton murdered all those girls?"

Everyone fell silent, though the low conversations of the surrounding people carried throughout the still air. One look toward the Schaeffers showed Clayton in the back seat of Detective Kendrick's unmarked state police vehicle, while Miles and Wes tried to reassure him that everything would be alright through the open window. It had been a nice gesture on Kendrick's part to allow such a conversation to take place at all.

"No, I don't believe Clay murdered Sophia or had anything else to do with those missing girls."

Lance tilted his head backward so that he could stare at the stars. The morning sun would be coming up over the horizon soon, dawning a new day. Would it begin with a fresh start, or would the past once again find a way to prevent them from moving on?

"This is just like what happened with Cassie and Darcy." Reese's summation drew everyone's attention her way. "I came to town seeking answers, and their reckless behavior made it seem as if they had something to do with Sophia's murder. In the end, they were only trying to protect Annie Osburn. It's the same with Clayton. He truly believed this investigation was going to be pinned on him because of the people and places he'd come across in his youth."

Cassie and Darcy's verdict had been delivered, and it appeared that both of them just barely skirted a jail sentence. The judge's compassion upon sentencing was most likely due to Reese's testimony that it was her wish the courts would show leniency due to the extenuating circumstances.

There was no difference in this situation, but that wasn't to say someone wasn't going to get hurt at some point in the near future.

"I'm afraid it's not going to stop here, either," Tiny chimed in, his displeasure evident over the fact that Brynn had gotten caught in the crosshairs. He took the words right out of her mouth, though. "Detective Kendrick, you need to find the son of a bitch who's turning our town inside out. It ain't right."

"We aren't pressing charges." Lance squeezed Brynn's hand as he made the announcement. Relief washed over her upon hearing his decision. Unfortunately, Detective Kendrick was no closer to finding out who murdered Sophia and Whitney than he was in solving Emma's disappearance. "There was no damage done other than that asshole killing my lawn. The firemen watered down the gasoline, so there isn't any more danger of a fire."

No damage? Brynn winced when she saw the injury she'd caused to Clayton's cheek with the key she'd had clutched in her hand. Yes, he deserved it—and more—for pursuing her through the yard and making her think he'd come there to kill her. Unfortunately, panic and desperation caused people to react recklessly and to make poor choices.

"The district attorney will be deciding on the validity of prosecuting this case. Your wish to let the culprit take a pass is not up to you. She can press charges in a felony crime, if she deems there is enough evidence to convict. I'll see if I can't express your wishes, though." Detective Kendrick then turned to Rose. "Mrs. Phifer, I don't want you to take this wrong way, but you and I need to have a more in-depth conversation regarding the residents in this town and their connection to the camp."

Tiny straightened his back, leveraging his height and displaying his displeasure at the fact that his wife was being dragged into this investigation. Brynn wasn't surprised when Rose stroked his arm in reassurance and agreed to be of whatever help needed in the coming days, weeks, or months it took to catch whoever had brought this evil amongst them.

The detective set up a time tomorrow to speak with Rose and Tiny, while Miles had finally made his way over to Gus. The two men shook hands while Miles apologized for the behavior of his son. Reese had hopped off the tailgate and joined Noah, who was speaking with Byron Warner about the possibility of Mitch running for sheriff.

In the distance, Brynn could see Deputy Foster and Byron dealing with the two media crews that had gotten wind of what had transpired this evening. The red and blue lights swirling above their vehicles on the bars weren't as bright as they once were as the morning sun finally made an appearance.

Even though charges might not be pressed against Clayton, he wouldn't escape being processed down at the station nor would he miss being thoroughly questioned by Detective Kendrick. There was no denying his presence at both crime scenes. Maybe he could remember something to help the investigation, though chances were small of that happening.

"There are too many secrets, aren't there?"

Lance wrapped his arm around Brynn, bringing with his embrace the security she now craved. She rested her cheek against the soft fabric of his shirt, grateful that she could still smell the strong odor of gasoline. It was the strangest thing to appreciate, but it meant they were still alive.

"Everyone has skeletons in their closet, some deeper than others." Brynn had things she didn't discuss about her parents, and Lance wasn't completely open about his time in the service.

The key was knowing their loved ones would be there should the day ever come when their secrets saw the light of day. "Clayton will have his family, and in a way…us. Making a few poor decisions doesn't make one a bad person."

"You and I both know Clayton was one step away from crossing that line."

"But he didn't take that step," Brynn reminded Lance, comfortable with the fact that he already looked inside her closet. This town represented her family, and she couldn't bring herself to accept that any of them could be guilty of something so horrific. "Oh, I didn't get to thank you."

"Thank me?" Lance questioned in surprise, pulling away just enough so he could figure out what she was talking about. "If you hadn't gone around the back of the house and screamed my name, I'd most likely be ashes right now."

"Oh, ye of little faith." Brynn reached up and pressed her palm against the whiskers on his face that had formed overnight. Couldn't he see that she wasn't talking about him coming outside with a shotgun? Apparently not. "Lance, I'm thanking you for staying by my side. You could have easily talked to Clay without standing on the spot that was saturated with gasoline."

"I hate to break this to you, but you're not getting rid of me that easily. I've loved you since the first time I saw you in Mrs. Sanders' math class back in ninth grade." Lance smiled, bringing with it a mischievous sparkle radiating from his blue eyes. "You're stuck with me. I left once before. I'm not leaving you ever again, blondie."

CHAPTER TWENTY-FIVE

One week later...

"**D**ID YOU HEAR about Clayton and Wes?"

Lance didn't look up from his cue stick, having the perfect lineup to sink the eight ball. He gently drew back the cue and followed through until the chalked tip connected with the cue ball in a perfectly choreographed moment of precision movements.

And...the eight ball gracefully moved across the table and sank in the left corner pocket he'd called a few seconds prior.

He smiled. His job here was done.

The Cavern was crowded this Friday night and the live band was in full swing. The lead singer had been encouraging the ladies to line dance all evening and had finally been successful in getting more than a few of the available women to line up, even bagging a couple of the men wanting to impress their dates.

"Yeah, I heard."

Lance couldn't say he wasn't glad that Clayton Schaeffer decided to head back to the city while he awaited the district attorney's decision on the plea deal his defense attorney had proposed. He might still manage to end up doing community service instead of jail time.

As it stood, the two older brothers had decided to give up the contract to build the new cottages up at the lake. Some of the townsfolk weren't as forgiving as Brynn had been, but most of them had followed her lead. In the end, it didn't matter to more than a few folks here in town. Clayton was his own worst enemy. He was having trouble excusing his own behavior, let alone expecting others to follow suit.

"It was probably for the best that he headed back to the city. Tensions around here don't seem too forgiving, if you get my drift. And hey, you got a damn good job out of it, too."

"That I did." Noah raised his beer in celebration, though Lance understood more than anyone that this wasn't the way he'd wanted to go into his partnership with Miles and Chad. "Rose agreed to Miles' terms in regard to the projected end date. We start first thing Monday morning. The inspection will still require a journey electrician to sign off on at least the first cottage, but I should have my state license by the time we start the second one."

Lance took a seat at the high-top table, waiting for Noah to begin racking the balls for another game. He never did like to lose. Two out of three it was.

A rather distinctive laugh came from one of the corner booths. Lance didn't have to look that way to know it was Harlan Whitmore. The real estate agent had been hitting the hard stuff pretty regularly since his interview, especially now after Calvin's heart attack and Clayton's fucked up decision to try and torch Lance's house.

Lance casually observed the other patrons, both at the tables and bar. Brynn wasn't back from the phone call she'd answered on her cell earlier. She'd gone to her office for some peace and quiet. He wasn't the hovering type, but he couldn't bring himself to let her lock up by herself after closing time any longer. It made for some long nights, but he didn't mind in the least.

Things could change once Detective Kendrick made an arrest, but Lance didn't see that happening any time soon. He didn't mind the adjustment to their schedules. As a matter of fact, he and his dad had gotten used to tag teaming certain projects. It was working out well, and Lance wasn't inclined to change a thing.

"Didn't you say Jace is coming home next week?" Reese asked, tossing a peanut shell back into the bowl. It was only the second time she'd spoken in the last hour. She'd had her nose practically pressed to the screen of her phone, searching for God knows what on the Internet. It was a wonder she could even focus her eyes on them when she inquired about Jace. "Did your dad mention what property Jace will get the keys to...maybe the Stoll farm to the west of town?"

"Do I even want to know what you're researching over there?" Noah walked around the table until he was standing behind Reese, doing his best to look over her shoulder to catch a glimpse of her cell phone. "Is that—"

"Tobias Essinger?" Reese finished the name Noah seemed to choke on. Her raised eyebrow told Lance she'd found something interesting. He took a seat at the table as well, double checking to see if Brynn had returned to the bar. She hadn't, which only gave her another minute before he sought her out. "Did you know that he used to do inspections on worksites?"

"Reese, you're going down that road again," Lance warned, sharing a look with Noah that said nothing good could come from them playing amateur detectives. "Tobias is lucky he has the strength to carry those western novels around that he likes so much. He wouldn't have been able to physically abduct Whitney, let alone kill her."

"No, but *he* would."

Noah already had a front row seat, having rested his palms on either side of Reese so he could lean in closer as she pointed to the display on her phone. Lance all but scrambled around the table. Could she have found something that Detective Kendrick missed? It was doubtful, but at this point, anything was possible.

"Wait," Lance cautioned, slowly taking the cell phone out of Reese's hand. He studied the man's face, having seen him before. "I remember this guy. He's—"

"Harold Burke." Noah rested a hand on Reese's shoulder, drawing her attention toward him while Lance read the article associated with the picture. "Sweetheart, I hate to break this to you, but that man is dead."

Reese might have stumbled onto a roadblock, but that didn't mean she wasn't headed in the right direction. Harold Burke had been a state certified housing inspector who helped Tobias out once in a while on the bigger jobs back in the day...but he hadn't been the only one.

"Give Detective Kendrick a call," Lance suggested, handing Reese back her phone. "He most likely has already checked out this lead, but you might be onto something. Harold Burke wasn't the only city inspector to help out old Tobias."

Talking about who could be responsible for such horrific murders had Lance searching for Brynn. She'd yet to come back from the phone call she'd taken in her office.

"I'll be right back."

Lance didn't stop to make small talk with those who tried to grab his attention. As for the media crews, only one news anchor and his cameraman were still in town. That group just happened to still be able to drink at the Cavern, though Brynn was keeping them on a tight leash. Charlene Winston hadn't been seen since Tiny had kicked her out of the Cavern a couple of weeks ago.

"She's still in her office."

Now that statement caught Lance's attention enough to slow his steps. Irish was resting his forearms atop a high table waiting for Chad to finish his round at the dart board. There was nothing in his demeanor that would have told any civilian he'd served in the military, but Lance wasn't a noncombatant.

"What branch?"

Irish didn't reply right away, but instead took a draw on the beer bottle in his hand. The delayed response told Lance this man wasn't comfortable sharing details of his past. Blue eyes clashed with one another as this newcomer all but made it known he wasn't in the mood to chat.

"Lance, good to see you." Chad joined Irish at the table, unaware of the slight tension. He reached for his beer. "I hear Jace is coming home next week."

"Yeah, that's the word," Lance replied cautiously, still scrutinizing the stranger who seemed to blend right in without anyone questioning his presence. "Chad, I might need you to look at something out at the house. Maybe you could drop by next week."

"Sure, I can swing around your place Monday morning."

Irish carefully set his beer on the table, his cautious gaze sliding from Lance toward the hallway leading to Brynn's office.

"It looks like it's my turn." Irish slapped the surface of the table, signifying it was time to bring this uncomfortable conversation to an end. "Schaeffer, you're about to buy the next round."

Lance had questions, but it looked as if they wouldn't be answered until Monday morning. He excused himself and made his way down the small hallway toward Brynn's office. Not bothering to knock, he twisted the doorknob and walked inside.

"…see you soon. Drive safe."

"Who will we see soon?" Lance closed the door behind him, drowning out the bass reverberating through the floorboards. Concern washed over him at the worry written across her beautiful features. "Blondie? What's going on?"

"That was Shae Irwin," Brynn replied, almost as if she didn't believe it herself. She even glanced down at her cell phone for confirmation. "She's coming home."

"Home, home?"

Lance needed more clarification on that account, because it sounded as if Shae was moving back to Blyth Lake. He wasn't so sure that was a good idea after what happened with Whitney. Granted, Shae's picture wasn't in the tin he'd found in his basement, but it had been her sister that had gone missing twelve years ago.

"Sorry," Brynn said with a quick shake of her head. He made his way around the desk and offered her his hand. "What I mean is she's been getting updates from Detective Kendrick, but she wants to be here herself. She said she hasn't been able to sleep, she's been losing weight, and she's constantly calling the detective for updates. Shae's driving herself crazy, so she's cleared her schedule and is taking a leave of absence from the hospital."

Lance heard through the grapevine that Shae had become some type of psychologist or psychiatrist, living in a state up north. He couldn't recall the details. Not that it mattered. He would most likely feel the need to be close to the investigation if this were about one of his siblings.

He pulled Brynn into his arms and held her tight without saying another word. She, Julie, and Emma had been almost inseparable back in the day. Losing Emma had been hard on everyone, but she'd been like a sister to Brynn...who'd already lost her parents. There was only so much loss a person could take.

"I told Shae she could stay upstairs in the apartment while she's here."

It took a moment for Lance to get the significance of what

Brynn was saying as she disclosed some of the discussion she'd had with Shae.

"If you're not—"

Lance hadn't realized how long he'd remained silent as her declaration finally sunk into his thick head. There wasn't a chance in hell she was changing her mind now.

He kissed her, cutting off whatever she'd been going to say because he'd been too shocked to reply. The two of them had been splitting their time between their respective places, though more and more they spent the night at the house…their house.

"We can start packing your stuff right now," Lance whispered, going in for another taste. She was as sweet as the Classic Coke she'd been drinking earlier. "The bed of my truck is empty, so it won't take me more than a couple trips."

Brynn gave a throaty laugh, wrapping her arms around his neck and standing on her tiptoes.

"I love you, Lance Kendall."

"That's good, because as I said before…you're stuck with me."

Lance had driven into town after twelve years away, but there'd been something special missing in the welcoming he'd experienced—Brynn Mercer.

She'd been right when she said they couldn't change the past, but what she didn't understand was that he wouldn't have altered a second about the years they'd spent together or the decade they'd spent apart. Every day after had led to this moment.

"Let's go home, blondie."

~ The End ~

Thank you for joining me in the Kendall family's journey. The mystery is still ongoing, and you're not going to want to miss the next installment in the Keys to Love series—Unlocking Lies!

www.kennedylayne.com/keys-to-love-book-three-mdash-unlocking-lies.html

Secrets and lies have a way of weaving a deadly web. Returning home from his last deployment shouldn't have been complicated, but Jace Kendall was immediately drawn into a murder investigation that hits a little too close to home. The last thing he should be doing was reigniting old passions that should have been kept buried, but he's never been a guy who plays by the rules.

Shae has suffered for twelve years without knowing why her sister disappeared. The long-awaited answers are now within reach, and she'll have no choice but to trust the one man who knows more than he's telling.

It isn't long before Jace and Shae are lost in the mystery of solving a case that's long gone cold. When they find the answers they've been looking for, a darkness is unveiled that will leave one of them in the crosshairs of a psychopath.

Books by Kennedy Layne

Keys to Love Series
Unlocking Fear (Keys to Love, Book One)
Unlocking Secrets (Keys to Love, Book Two)
Unlocking Lies (Keys to Love, Book Three)
Unlocking Shadows (Keys to Love, Book Four)
Unlocking Darkness (Keys to Love, Book Five)

Surviving Ashes Series
Essential Beginnings (Surviving Ashes, Book One)
Hidden Ashes (Surviving Ashes, Book Two)
Buried Flames (Surviving Ashes, Book Three)
Endless Flames (Surviving Ashes, Book Four)
Rising Flames (Surviving Ashes, Book Five)

CSA Case Files Series
Captured Innocence (CSA Case Files 1)
Sinful Resurrection (CSA Case Files 2)
Renewed Faith (CSA Case Files 3)
Campaign of Desire (CSA Case Files 4)
Internal Temptation (CSA Case Files 5)
Radiant Surrender (CSA Case Files 6)
Redeem My Heart (CSA Case Files 7)

Red Starr Series

Starr's Awakening & Hearths of Fire (Red Starr, Book One)
Targets Entangled (Red Starr, Book Two)
Igniting Passion (Red Starr, Book Three)
Untold Devotion (Red Starr, Book Four)
Fulfilling Promises (Red Starr, Book Five)
Fated Identity (Red Starr, Book Six)
Red's Salvation (Red Starr, Book Seven)

The Safeguard Series

Brutal Obsession (The Safeguard Series, Book One)
Faithful Addiction (The Safeguard Series, Book Two)
Distant Illusions (The Safeguard Series, Book Three)
Casual Impressions (The Safeguard Series, Book Four)
Honest Intentions (The Safeguard Series, Book Five)
Deadly Premonitions (The Safeguard Series, Book Six)

About the Author

First and foremost, I love life. I love that I'm a wife, mother, daughter, sister... and a writer.

I am one of the lucky women in this world who gets to do what makes them happy. As long as I have a cup of coffee (maybe two or three) and my laptop, the stories evolve themselves and I try to do them justice. I draw my inspiration from a retired Marine Master Sergeant that swept me off of my feet and has drawn me into a world that fulfills all of my deepest and darkest desires. Erotic romance, military men, intrigue, with a little bit of kinky chili pepper (his recipe), fill my head and there is nothing more satisfying than making the hero and heroine fulfill their destinies.

Thank you for having joined me on their journeys...

Email:

kennedylayneauthor@gmail.com

Facebook:

facebook.com/kennedy.layne.94

Twitter:

twitter.com/KennedyL_Author

Website:

www.kennedylayne.com

Newsletter:

www.kennedylayne.com/newsletter.html

CPSIA information can be obtained
at www.ICGtesting.com
Printed in the USA
LVOW10s0259110418
573059LV00024B/1154/P